LOST & FOUND

Five people.Three stories. New beginnings.

Lily Van Allen

PUBLISHED BY

SIGMA'S
BOOKSHELF

MINNETONKA, MN 55305
WWW.SIGMASBOOKSHELF.COM

Dedication

This book is dedicated to my best friend Mira, who edited all the short stories I wrote prior to this book, and inspired me to write more.

Part 1

The Six-year-old Boy

Chapter 1

Lorraine Sky

September 20, 1982

"Name?"

"Excuse me?" I asked, turning around.

"Miss, what is your name?"

"Oh, of course. Sorry! My name is Lorraine Sky," I said to the young woman sitting behind the counter.

"Welcome Ms. Sky. Detective Grayson will see you in a few minutes. He's stuck in a meeting right now. You can sit down in the waiting area," she said, gesturing to a corner with a few chairs in it. I perched on a floral chair and adjusted my glasses. I then took out my book, *A Day in Summer* by J.L. Carr, and read for a while.

After about 20 minutes, I dog-eared my page and checked my watch. It has been long enough, I thought, as I stood up and walked to the desk.

"Excuse me, miss, but shouldn't Grayson be out of his meeting by now?" I asked.

"He's still in his meeting, Ms. Sky. Please go sit down in the waiting area," she said, pointing to the corner.

"Can you please contact him? Can you please tell him I'm here?"

"Ma'am, your problem is not a priority to him at the present moment."

"Excuse me? My son is missing! How is this not a priority at the present moment?"

"Elise, can you get Robby on the-" Grayson started, walking into the dim lobby of the police station.

"Good morning, Andy," I scoffed, glaring at him.

"Lorraine! I wasn't expecting you this early!"

"Yeah right! Care to explain why my son isn't a priority?"

"Lorraine, let's talk in my office," he said, leading me down the hallway. He closed his office door and sat down at his desk.

"What makes a missing child not a priority?"

"Lorraine, Joey is probably with a family member. That's what happens with most missing children."

"Andy! I am Joey's only family! There has to be something you can do!"

"Lorraine," he sighed, "you're not his only family."

"Yes I am his only family! My parents abandoned me when I joined The Peace Corps!"

"Lorraine! I am his father! He is OUR son!" he shouted, grabbing my arms with his hands. He was shaking me back and forth as if he thought that would help me absorb that fact.

"Joey doesn't know you exist! He doesn't know anything about his dad! He doesn't even need a father. I'm doing just fine with him!"

"He needs a father, Lorraine."

"No, he does not! And again, he does not know you exist!"

"Well, maybe you should have told him who I am!"

"Maybe you shouldn't have cheated on me!" I cried, taking a step away from him.

"Don't make this about me!"

"Why not? You're such a coward, Andy! Just think, if you

hadn't gone off and cheated, we'd be perfectly happy right now! You, me, and Joey!"

"In that ratty old house of yours? No thank you ma'am!"

"Please, Andy. Help me get Joey back."

"Fine," he sighed. "I'll see what I can do." I smiled and left.

When I reached my house, I climbed out of my rusty old car and slammed the front door of my house, which caused plaster to fall from the ceiling. I sighed and leaned against the door with my eyes closed. Suddenly, the phone started to ring. I jumped up and ran to answer it.

"Hello?" I asked, trying to untangle the cord.

"Lorraine, it's Andy. We need you to come back to the station."

"What happened? Did you find him? Did you find something?" I asked, shaking.

"Just come back down to the station in that rusty old car of yours. I'll meet you outside."

"I'll be right there," I said, hanging up the phone. I grabbed my car keys and drove down to the station yet again.

When I got to the station, I saw Andy smoking a cigarette on the sidewalk. I climbed out my car and he stomped it out when he saw me.

"We need to know what happened to you and Joey on the night he was taken."

"Oh, of course," I said, glad that he was finally expressing interest in the fact that our son was missing.

"Come on in," he said, holding the door open for me. He led me down a dimly lit hallway and into a dark room with a metal table and two chairs.

"An interrogation room? Really Andy?"

"People are more honest when we talk to them in here. Please, sit down," he said, pulling out one of the chairs for me. It was made of metal as well. I set my purse on the table.

"So, what questions do you have for me?"

"What's your real last name?"

"Andy, what kind of question is that?"

"Just answer the question Lorraine!" he barked, banging his fist on the table.

"My real name is Lorraine Cochrane."

"Where are you originally from Ms. Cochrane?"

"I'm from East Hampton, New York."

"And what are you doing in the small town of Magnolia, West Virginia, Ms. Cochrane? That must have been a big change."

"When I was in high school, my parents abandoned me because I wanted to join the Peace Corps. I left East Hampton. I left my family's piles of money, and I traveled the world with a suitcase and a notebook in which I kept track of my adventures. I stayed in the Corps for two years before discovering Magnolia. Let's just say I fell in love in more than one way. I moved here, and I met a scrawny rookie detective and we got married two months later. A year after that we had a little baby boy, and then five months later, my husband cheated on me and I divorced him."

"How old was your son when he was kidnapped?"

"He was five. He'll be six in two weeks."

"What was the date of his kidnapping?"

"Friday, September 16, 1982," I mumbled, tearing up. Andy reached his hand across the table and gently held mine.

"We're gonna find Joey, okay?" he whispered, smiling at me.

"What other questions do you have?"

"There's one question left. This one might be difficult. What happened Friday night?" he asked, looking me directly in the eyes.

"I-I can't answer that, Andy."

"You can do this. Once you answer the question, we're gonna find Joey."

"Can you get a sketch artist in here? I know what the kidnapper looks like."

"For now, just talk. I'll notify Ralph once this meeting is over."

"Okay," I said, taking a deep breath. "It was a cloudy night and extremely humid. Joey and I had come home late from choir practice at the church. Anyway, I was putting Joey in his bed when he asked me a question."

"What did he ask you?"

"H-he pointed to his bedroom door, which was open, and asked, 'Mommy, do you know that man behind the door?' I said he was tired because he was already dreaming. When I turned around to leave, I saw a man creeping out from behind the door. I tried to get to Joey, but in a split second, he was on top of me. He had knocked the wind out of me. I couldn't breathe, couldn't speak, couldn't move, but I could see."

"What did you see?"

"He was tall, 6'4" or 6'5" and he was wearing all black. He had on a hood which had fallen off. He had shaggy blond hair that looked like it hadn't been washed for months and yellow eyes like black cats in paintings. And his face, oh my God, his face!"

"What was wrong with his face?"

"He had this network of deep scars across the right side of his face, and his eyes were bloodshot, and his lips were chapped. His face seemed like it was glowing. And he said something to me."

"What did he say?"

"'You didn't forget what I told you, Lorraine, or did you?' and then he punched me. That man knocked me out."

"What happened when you woke up?"

"Joey was gone. He had taken him. And I could still hear his screams echoing in my ear."

"Did he hurt you in any way?"

"Yes, he did. There are bruises around my arms from where he was holding me down, and a bruise where he punched me."

"And what did you do after you woke up?"

"I called you," I said.

Andy sat back in his chair, deep in thought. I knew that face. I was practically married to that face.

"I'll call you when we have some leads," he finally said.

I got in my car and went back home. When I got inside, I put my keys on the telephone table and turned on my old radio. "Sweet Caroline" by Neil Diamond was playing. When we were married, Andy sang this song to me all the time while he was playing his guitar. I always joined in when it got to the chorus. Everyone said I was good enough to be a professional singer, but I was never adventurous enough to go out and do it. Andy said it was the biggest mistake I ever made, but I'm fine with it. If I went off to Hollywood instead of moving to Magnolia, I wouldn't have Joey, and a world without that little boy just kills me. Now that the nightmare is real, all I want to do is run away.

"Sweet Caroline," I softly sang, standing at the kitchen sink. I'm now the choir director at the church and I get paid an okay amount of money. It's enough to get by.

For the rest of the day, I cleaned the house. At six o'clock, the news came on and I stopped dead in my tracks. Al Glover, the town's prominent radio personality, was speaking.

"We have a special bulletin from the Magnolia Police Station. On Friday night, five-year-old Joseph Grayson, son of the church choir director Lorraine Sky, was kidnapped from his home. If you see the child or have any information on his disappearance, you are urged to contact the Magnolia Police Station immediately. I'm Al Glover, and we'll be right back after these messages," he said.

I finished cleaning, and then I began to make dinner when the doorbell rang. I walked into the front hallway and opened the door. Sherrie Anders, the pastor's wife, was on the porch.

"Good evening, Lorraine. Everyone at the church is real sorry about Joey. We all loved the boy like he was our own."

"Thank you for your thoughts, Sherrie."

"Here's a macaroni casserole. It's my secret recipe," she said, thrusting a pan toward me.

"Thank you, Sherrie."

"Goodbye, hun. See you soon. Hope you find Joey."

"Goodbye, Sherrie," I said, closing the front door. I set the casserole in a warming container and finished making dinner. As I pulled the casserole out, I heard a knock on the door.

"Hey, Lorraine. I just wanted to stop by and see if you were doing okay," Andy said after I opened the door.

"It was nice of you to think of me for once," I sighed, rolling my eyes.

"Look Lorraine, I'm real sorry about what I did. I guess I'll be going now."

"Andy wait. Do you want some dinner? Sherrie Anders brought over a macaroni casserole about 30 minutes ago. You wanna share it with me?"

"Sure, why not?" he shrugged, turning around. He sat down at the kitchen table and I set out a plate for him and walked to the fridge.

"You want a beer?" I asked.

"Sure."

I tossed a can of beer to him and sat down across from him.

"So, how are things with you?" I asked, trying to make normal conversation with the guy I hadn't talked to in five years.

"Well, after we got divorced, I bought a house across town,

not because I wanted to be far away from you, but because it was closer to the station. I guess I haven't done much of anything," he shrugged.

"Okay then. How nice is this house?"

"Not much nicer than this one to be honest. Looks like we've both got our ratty houses."

"And we love the crumbling plaster so much!" I joked.

"Hey! That's my favorite part!"

"Okay, let's cut the crap. Why did you cheat on me, Andy?"

"What kind of a question is that?"

"It's a perfectly reasonable question considering what you asked me this morning!"

"Those questions you answered are helping me find our son!"

"Answer the question, Andy!"

"Fine! You wanna know the answer? I didn't cheat on you! That woman was a wanted felon and I was in charge of arresting her! I never did anything!"

"How come you never told me?"

"Lorraine, I tried to tell you, but you wouldn't listen."

"I'm sorry I never listened to you. In a way, it's kind of like how we got together."

"You still remember that?"

"Andy, I remember everything."

"Oh my God, I was so nervous that night."

"I could tell," I said, resting my hand on his forearm. He smiled and took my hand in his.

Chapter 2

Seven Years Earlier, Andy Grayson

March 31, 1975

As I sat on the stoop of my apartment building smoking a cigarette, a bright blue Volkswagen beetle pulled up to the curb and a girl got out. She was the most beautiful woman I'd ever seen. She saw me staring and I nervously looked at the ground. She had dark brown hair, red lips, and piercing blue eyes.

I looked back up at her and she began to walk towards me. She was wearing a purple dress and a purple sweater. It was easy to tell that she wasn't from here.

"Excuse me. I don't mean to bother you, but could you please direct me to the Delancey Building?" she asked, holding her white purse in front of her.

"The Delancey Building?"

"Yes, the Delancey Building," she nodded, sliding her feet back and forth.

"Why, you're standing right in front of it! I'm sorry, you must be new here. Welcome to Magnolia Miss-"

"Lorraine Sky. Thank you for the welcome," she said,

shaking my hand. She pulled an old suitcase out of her car and walked back towards me.

"I'm Andy Grayson. Do you need help with moving your stuff?"

"No, thank you. I only have one bag," she muttered.

"So what brings you to Magnolia? You must've had a drastic change in your life to choose this small town," I said, following her up the stairs.

"You'll find out soon. It was very nice to meet you, Andy," she said. I smiled sheepishly and walked up the next flight of stairs as she unlocked her door.

I opened the door to my apartment and walked inside. Now that I was by myself, I grabbed a bottle of beer from my fridge. I sat on the couch and quietly began to sing "Ain't No Mountain High Enough" by Marvin Gaye and Tammi Terrell. Suddenly, I heard singing from the apartment below mine. Someone was singing "Strawberry Fields Forever" by The Beatles. I walked into the hallway as my best friend, Lewis, leaned out of his apartment.

"Who is that singing?" he asked, looking warily down the corridor.

"I dunno. Stay here. I'll go look," I reassured Lewis. I walked down the stairs, trying to decipher the voice. I'm good at that kind of stuff. Last year, I joined the police force, and within six months, I was the best detective at the station. When I got to the source of the singing, I knocked on the door.

"Hello? Oh, hi Andy. Is everything okay?" Lorraine asked, opening her door. I smiled nervously.

"Andy, is it safe?" Lewis asked from upstairs.

"Come on down, Lewis! Meet our new neighbor!" I shouted. Seconds later, Lewis clambered down the stairs and to Lorraine's door.

"Lorraine, this is my best friend, Lewis. If you hear any strange sounds coming from a piano, that's Lewis trying to 'find his sound.' Lewis, this is Lorraine. She just moved here."

"Nice to meet you, Miss Lorraine. And I'm a jazz pianist. That's what Andy The Ignorant means by 'finding my sound.'"

"It's nice to meet you, Lewis," Lorraine giggled.

"So, Lorraine, do you maybe want to go dancing tonight? There's a great band downtown," I said, scratching the back of my head.

"I would love that, Andy."

"Great! I'll pick you up at eight?"

"Sure. See you tonight."

"See you tonight!" I hollered, walking down the hallway with Lewis.

We walked into my apartment and he grabbed a beer from my fridge. He began to laugh.

"Dude, she just got here!" he hollered, still laughing.

"I think I may be in love," I sighed, sitting down on the couch.

"You met this girl not even 15 minutes ago. You only know her name, and you think you're ready to profess your love to her?"

"Yeah, what's so wrong with that?"

"How long have we been friends?"

"Since you moved here from Harlem when we were both nine."

"Right. And what did we promise each other?"

"To stop each other from doing stupid things. What's the purpose of this question?" I asked, looking up at Lewis. He banged his fists on my kitchen counter.

"This is a stupid thing! This is the most stupid thing you have ever done! Can't you get that into your brilliant mind?"

"Says the one who ran off to New Orleans after giving his valedictorian speech and not even staying three years."

"That's not what this is about! You can't tell a girl you just met that you love her! Don't you know that's the kind of thing you do to scare a girl off?"

"Well then, what am I supposed to do? Never talk to her again?"

"Go out with her you imbecile! Go on some dates. Learn everything about her! After a few months, tell her you love her! Girls like to take things slow," he said, sliding onto the couch. "You really are clueless for having a photographic memory."

"Oh shut up."

"Nope, good luck bud. I'll see you tomorrow."

"Crap, now I'm all alone," I sighed, standing up. I turned on my TV and watched football until about an hour before I had to go.

Eventually, I switched off the TV, took a shower, got dressed, and then practiced my dancing. I'm not the most graceful human being. I'm basically just a walking stick. I'm six-foot-six and the thing I do most is trip over my size 13 feet. I guess I can't change things now.

As the clock ticked, I rolled up the sleeves of my white dress shirt and pushed a tattered green hat on top of my shaggy black hair. At 7:59, I buckled my suspenders, put my shoes on, and walked down to Lorraine's apartment. I knocked on the door and took a deep breath.

"Hi, Andy. You look great," she said, stepping out of her apartment. She looked even more beautiful than this morning. She was now in a yellow dress with a red belt, red shoes, and her hair was tied up with a red ribbon.

"You look beautiful, Lorraine," I muttered, trying to muster as much confidence as I could. Lorraine giggled.

"Thanks Andy," she blushed as we walked outside.

That night was quite interesting. I tried to tell Lorraine how I felt, but she just kept talking, and not listening. I chased after her for a week and she finally began to listen.

Chapter 3

About A Month After the Kidnapping, Andy Grayson

October 25, 1982

I t has been more than one month since he disappeared, and there have been no new leads on Joey. Lorraine is falling apart. She rarely remembers the most trivial things, and without Joey it's like she can't function properly. So, we've been spending more time together, trying to connect. It has been nice spending time with her.

We know who the kidnapper is, a man with the alias Richard Cory, like in the poem by Edwin Arlington Robinson. There's only one problem. I just learned the Richard Cory we've been looking for is dead. He was killed ten years ago.

I've decided it's time to enlist the help of someone who can make the number of leads skyrocket. I slammed my car door shut and walked through the dead grass. I knocked on the front door.

"What do you want?" a weathered old man asked after opening the door.

"It's nice to see you too, Dad," I said, rolling my eyes.

I hooked my thumbs in the belt loops on my jeans and shifted my weight.

"Andrew. I didn't recognize you. Come on in," my father said, hobbling into my old house. Nothing had changed since I left eight years ago.

"So, what's up with you? How's that beautiful wife of yours? Lorraine, right?"

"We're divorced."

"Sorry."

"Dad, I need your help."

"What is it?" he asked, sitting down at the 100-year-old oak kitchen table.

"Joey's missing."

"Little Joey's missing? What happened to my only grandchild, Andrew?"

"He was kidnapped just over a month ago by an intruder in Lorraine's house. The entire town has been trying to help find him. Everyone except for you. Please Dad, we need your help."

"Andrew, I'm not going to help you."

"Why not Dad? I've never asked you for anything!"

"Because I am retired! I've seen too much crime, too much death, too many unthinkable things!" he shouted.

"Dad! You're Robert Grayson! You're the best detective this godforsaken town has ever seen! You solved cases faster than they took place!" I cried.

"Sure, I was good, but I can't go back. It's too hard."

"Please Dad. Please help me get my son back. Lorraine, she's a different person without him. She can't be by herself for more than a couple hours. Then she remembers he's gone."

"And what have you been doing to help her?"

"Everyone in town has been helping out. They've organized search parties, assemblies, benefits, all of them to help Lorraine."

"That's not what I'm asking. What have YOU been doing to help Lorraine?"

"I've been sleeping on her couch."

Chapter 4

Lorraine Sky

October 30, 1982

*A*s I drove through the streets of my hometown, the nostal-
gia of it all hit me hard. I waved to old friends walking
past the storefronts, and looked at the changing leaves
*of fall. I turned down one of the tree-lined lanes and drove to
the end of a luxury cul-de-sac. I parked my car in front of a
large stone manor and walked inside.*

*"As I live and breathe. Hey everybody! Lori's home!" Dorothea,
the head maid, exclaimed, giving me a hug.*

"Welcome home, doll," my father said, walking into the foyer.

*"It's great to see you, father. Where's Bobby?" I asked, giving
my father a hug. Dorothea took my suitcase and carried it up
the stairs.*

*"He should be around here somewhere. Robert! Your sister's
home from school!" father barked. A thin, blond-haired boy
came running into the foyer, followed by my mother.*

"It's great to see you, Lorraine," he said, giving me a hug.

"Welcome home, darling," my mother said.

*"Come into the dining room. It's almost time for dinner," my
father said, walking through a set of white doors. We all sat
down at a wooden dining table, and dinner was served.*

"So, honey, how's school going?" my mother asked.

"It's okay, but I don't think it's for me," I shrugged. My father almost broke his glass of chardonnay.

"What do you mean you don't think it's for you? What else could you possibly want to do?"

"Mother, father, Bobby, I'm joining the Peace Corps."

I couldn't even begin to describe what happened next.

"Lorraine Maria Cochrane, get out of my house! As of right now, I have no daughter!" my father bellowed after a string of obscenities.

I looked at him accusingly and ran out of the dining room. I grabbed my suitcase from my bedroom and ran out of the house.

"That's right! Go away! Don't come back! I hope you live an unhappy life, Lorraine, and if I find out you're doing perfectly fine, I'm not afraid to take away the source of your happiness! Even if that includes killing someone!" Bobby cried as I ran out of the house. I got one last look at him before I sped off. I looked directly in his yellow eyes and saw the pure hatred in them.

I woke up in a cold sweat. I was back in my room, and Andy was shaking me back and forth, trying desperately to wake me up.

"Andy!" I cried, giving him a hug.

"What happened?" he asked, hugging me back.

"I know who has Joey."

"Who?"

"My brother."

"Why your brother?"

"The dream I just had was about the night I got kicked out of my house. On the night Joey was taken, the kidnapper repeated what Bobby said to me the night I left for the Peace Corps. Bobby has my son. Oh my God. What if he's dead?" I cried.

"Joey's not dead, Lorraine. We're gonna find him."

"But Bobby said he would do anything to keep me from being happy, even if that meant killing someone."

"Get dressed. We're going downtown," Andy said, letting go of me.

"I can remember the first time you said that."

"The night we got married."

"Andy, there's something I need to tell-" I started.

"Can it wait, Lorraine?"

"I guess it has to," I mumbled, getting up. Andy went downstairs and dialed the phone.

"Elise, get everyone down to the station. There's been a break in the case," I heard him say from downstairs.

Chapter 5

Lorraine Sky

June 8, 1975

As Andy and I sat in his small living room listening to the radio, he grew fidgety. I turned the radio off. "Andy, are you okay? You seem off," I said.

"You wanna get married?"

"What are you talking about?"

"You wanna get married, like, right now?"

"Andy, that's crazy! We've only known each other for two months!"

"But we fell in love in one night. Come on Lorraine... I love you, you love me, and we could make each other so happy! Just think, we can get a house out in the country, like that old Keats farm, and we can have four little kids running around and having fun. Come on Lorraine. Let's get married."

"Andy, we don't have a ring!"

"Oh yes we do. My Pa gave me his wedding bands when I moved out. He told me to save them for the woman I love more than anything. That woman is you, Lorraine."

"I don't know what to say, Andy."

"Wait here just a second and close your eyes," he said. I sat down on the couch and closed my eyes.

He put a record on. It was "Sweet Caroline" by Neil Diamond.

"Okay, open your eyes," he whispered.

I opened my eyes to see him kneeling on the floor in front of me, holding and old wedding band in his hand.

"Andy -"

"Lorraine Cochrane, I still know the exact moment I fell in love with you because you are the only person I know who would ever sing 'Strawberry Fields Forever' when they're alone. Lorraine, you're the only woman I will ever love, so will you make me the happiest man to ever live and marry me?" he asked, his hand shaking.

"Yes! I'll marry you!" I cried as he slipped the ring onto my finger. He hoisted me up into the air and began to sing along with the record.

That same afternoon, we raced off to the church with Lewis in the back seat and pulled up just as Mr. Anders was locking the doors.

"Mr. Anders! We need to get married right now!" I cried.

"It's that much of a necessity? Is there something you kids aren't telling me?" he asked, turning to face us.

"No, sir. We just really want to get married right now," Andy said.

"Well, come on in. I'll have to get the courthouse on the phone so you have get a marriage license."

"That's no problem, sir," I sighed.

"Yes, good evening Janine. I know it's late, but I have two great kids here who want a marriage license ASAP. Their names are Andrew Grayson and Lorraine Sky."

"Well?" Lewis asked. He's not good with spontaneity.

"Janine will be right over with the license. Come on, let's go into the chapel," he said, unlocking the doors. We walked down the aisle hand in hand and stood at the front with Mr. Anders between us and Lewis behind Andy.

"Dearly Beloved, we are gathered here today to celebrate the union of Lorraine Sky and Andrew Grayson. May I have the rings? Andrew, do you take Lorraine to be your lawfully wedded wife in sickness and in health, till death do you part?"

"I do," Andy said, smiling at me as he slid the ring on my finger.

"And do you, Lorraine, take Andrew to be your lawfully wedded husband in sickness and in health, till death do you part?"

"I do," I whispered, sliding the ring on to his finger.

"I now pronounce you husband and wife. Andrew, you may now kiss your bride," he announced, stepping aside. That was the single greatest night of my life right there.

Chapter 6

Lorraine Sky

October 30, 1982

A s Andy and I sped off to the station, we were joined by a fleet of cars heading in the same direction. It seemed as if everyone who had been helping us with the case was answering the call to come to the station.

When we arrived, we ran inside the station only to be met by Andy's dad, hobbling down the dingy hallway with his cane.

"What in God's name is this commotion about?" he asked.

"Lorraine knows who took Joey."

"It's a pleasure to see you again, Mr. Grayson," I said, giving the old man a hug. Joey hadn't met him either.

"You look wonderful, Lorraine. Now, let's get your son back," he muttered, leading the congregation of exhausted police officers and civilians who had come in after us.

"So, who's the lucky fugitive?" Mr. Grayson asked.

"My brother," I said. Suddenly, I was bombarded with questions. I answered each one with ease.

"Okay, we'll contact you when we get a location on the kidnapper," one of the officers stated, closing his notebook.

"Excuse me?" I asked, stepping towards the lanky officer.

"We'll contact you when we get more leads, ma'am."

"How dare you speak to me like that! My six-year-old son is missing! My own brother has him, and he could've killed Joey by now! I am NOT going home!" I shouted, pushing the officer backwards.

"Lorraine, let's go," Andy muttered, taking my hand.

"I'm not going anywhere!" I cried, falling into Andy's arms. I broke down in tears and fell to his feet.

"Come on, Lorraine. You need rest. I'll take you to my office," Andy whispered, helping me up. He led me down the hallway and he told me to sit down on his couch. I did and he covered me with a blanket. Soon enough, I fell fast asleep. When I woke up, Andy was reading at his desk.

"Good morning, sleepyhead," he said, flashing his mischievous smile.

"How long was I asleep?"

"About five hours, and no, there haven't been any leads."

"I miss Joey so much. I just wish he was here and I could hold him in my arms and sing to him."

"I wish I could do that too."

Chapter 7

Andy Grayson

September 29, 1976

As sunlight streamed into my bedroom, I heard Lorraine softly muttering my name.

"Andy... Andy..."

"Good morning sweetie, how's our little baby?" I asked, kissing her cheek. Lorraine is now 8 1/2 months pregnant with our first child.

"My water just broke."

"Oh crap. This is happening."

"Why would this be bad? Just think, soon, we'll be on the way home with a little baby. Oh crap, this *is* happening. Hurry, get the bag and let's get in the car!" she cried as I helped her out of bed.

Lorraine doubled over in pain thanks to what I'm guessing was the first contraction. I quickly led her down the stairs and we headed to the hospital, which we got to in minutes.

"Excuse me ma'am!"

"Yes?" the nurse at the front desk asked.

"My wife is in labor!"

"We need a wheelchair over here!" the nurse hollered. Two other nurses rushed over with a wheelchair and I rushed into a room with them.

33 long hours later, we had a baby boy, and Lorraine was exhausted. I held her hand the entire time and I was still holding it now.

"Here's your baby boy," a nurse whispered, carrying my son into the room. I took him in my arms and we listened to the radio. He gurgled happily when "New York State of Mind" came on. I started singing along.

"You like this, don't you? When you're a big boy, your momma and I will teach you how to play like Billy Joel does," I whispered as he grabbed onto my pointer finger with his tiny hands.

"Aw, look at my two favorite boys bonding," Lorraine said, sitting up.

"I promised we'd teach him how to play piano and sing like Billy Joel," I whispered, gently handing him to Lorraine.

"I bet we could manage that. So, what are we gonna name our little music lover, huh?" she asked. I leaned back and lifted my foot, which caused Lorraine's bag to tumble over. On the floor was Lorraine's favorite book, *A Day in Summer* by J.L. Carr. I picked it up and looked at her, shaking my head.

"You really can't live without this book, can you?"

"It's my favorite book! What's so wrong with that?"

"Nothing, it's just kind of funny," I said, putting the book back in her bag. Suddenly, our little boy began to sob uncontrollably. I silently checked off hygiene, food, and music; and then I realized what he was crying about. Our son loved the book. I picked it up again and set it against the radio. Lorraine gaped at me, awestruck.

"How did you figure that out?"

"Photographic memory, my love, it's all thanks to the photographic memory," I said, tapping my temple. Lorraine laughed.

"So, little guy, what's your name gonna be?"

"What did you say the first two initials of J.L. Carr's name were?"

"Joseph Lloyd," she said. The baby began to giggle.

"Do you like that name? Joseph Lloyd Grayson. Does that sound good?"

"That sounds wonderful. Welcome to Magnolia, Joseph Lloyd," Lorraine whispered as our little boy fell asleep. This was my family. My wonderful, amazing little family.

Chapter 8

Lorraine Sky

October 31, 1982

I stood up and walked to Andy's desk. "Halloween is Joey's favorite holiday. Just before Bobby took him, we were getting ready to make his costume. He was gonna be a robot. They were having a costume contest at his school, and he wanted to win. He really wanted to win."

"We'll get him back, Lorraine. Don't you worry about it. So, what did you want to tell me last night?"

"Oh, nevermind. It's nothing," I shrugged, trying my best to hide my emotion. Suddenly, two deputy officers came bursting in.

"Boss! We have a location on the suspect!" one of them shouted.

"Oh my God. Joey! My Joey!" I cried, my hands shaking.

"Come on, Lorraine. Let's get our son back," Andy said, taking my hand. We sprinted to his car as rain lightly fell from the sky.

"Okay, Martinez. Where are we going?"

"The old Keats farm off Sycamore," Deputy Officer Martinez, my next-door-neighbor said over the intercom. A fleet of cop cars pulled out in front of us. Mr. Grayson was leading the procession.

"You wanna tell the boys anything to look out for?" Andy asked, holding out the microphone for the intercom.

"Hey guys, this is Lorraine. When we get to the house, let me coax Bobby out. Don't use your guns unless absolutely necessary, or else Joey will get scared, and let's bring my boy home!"

"Don't worry, Miss Lorraine. We've got your back," an officer said over the intercom. A chorus of voices echoed in agreement.

We drove out of town and finally parked on the grass of an old shotgun house. We all quietly got out and I picked up a rock and looked at Andy. He nodded in approval, and I threw the rock into the last intact window, shattering it. The door opened and the officers closed in on the house. Bobby bounded out of the house, expecting juveniles to be the ones who threw the rock. He saw the police officers and tried to get back inside, but Andy, who was on the porch, had closed the door and was standing in front of it.

"What do you scumbags-" he started.

"Robert Cochrane, you're under arrest for the kidnapping of Joseph Grayson, as well as breaking and entering, and the assault of Lorraine Sky."

"What? I didn't-"

"Didn't do what? Threaten me, stalk me and my family, break into my house, assault me, take away the person I care about the most? You can shut up right now, Bobby. It's over. You lost," I said, walking through the crowd. Bobby gasped.

"Lorraine-"

"What? You didn't think I'd be here to get my son back? You deserve to be dead. You know that, right? We're going easy on you."

"I didn't do anything that-"

"Do you really think I didn't tell them all about what

you said to me before I left home? Trust me, you deserve to be dead."

Just then, Mr. Grayson walked over and put the handcuffs on Bobby and said, "Robert Cochrane, you're under arrest for burglary, breaking and entering, assault, and kidnapping. You have the right to an attorney-"

"Really? You're having this old fart arrest me? Lorraine, I thought you were smarter than that," he choked, struggling to get free.

"That, you insolent bag of crap, is my father, and the greatest detective this town has ever had," Andy said, walking off the porch.

"Where's the kid?" Mr. Grayson asked.

"What?"

"Where's my son, Bobby?"

"I ain't telling you."

"Well then, I guess I'll just have to find him myself," Mr. Grayson sighed, shoving Bobby into the back seat of a car. Two deputy officers got in and drove off.

"Mr. Grayson, you don't have to-"

"Lorraine, let me get your son back."

"Mr. Grayson-"

"Please Lorraine! My name is Robert, and I'm going to get your son. Andrew, make sure Lorraine stays here."

"Yes, dad," Andy said, pulling me into his arms.

"W-what if he's not in there?" I whispered.

"He's in there, Lorraine. I can feel it," Andy muttered. I dug my head into Andy's shoulder and everyone held their breath until the door opened.

I looked up and saw Robert walking out of the house with someone. It was Joey. I breathed a sigh of relief and began to cry.

"Mommy!" Joey cried, running into my arms.

"Oh, I missed you so much baby," I sighed, picking him

up. I cradled him on my hip and he gave me a kiss on the cheek.

"I missed you too, mommy."

"Come on, I want you to meet someone," I said, setting Joey on the ground. He took my hand and I led him towards Andy. "Joey, this is your daddy."

"Hi Daddy."

"Hey bud. You've gotten so big since I last saw you!" Andy said, kneeling in the damp grass. Joey ran into his arms. Andy stood up and carried him to the car and set him in the back seat. As we drove off, the rain began to get heavier until it was a downpour.

When we pulled up in front of the house, I got out of the car quickly, opened the back door and grabbed Joey, then dodging raindrops ran him inside. After I set down my smiling child, I looked out the window and was surprised to see Andy walking to his car. I ran towards him and said, "Where do you think you're going?"

"Well, he's back, I'll leave you alone again," he announced.

"You were right! He does need a father!" I shouted over the deafening raindrops.

"What do you mean by that?" he asked.

"I still love you, stupid!"

"I still love you too-"

"Shut up and kiss me, you idiot!"

Chapter 9

Lorraine Sky

July 17, 1985

I was driving through the streets of my hometown again, but this time it was different. This time, I had a family. A couple months after Joey came back, Andy and I got remarried in a small church wedding, almost exactly like the first time, and we now have a baby girl named Alexandra. We were all back in East Hampton to visit my parents.

Andy parked the car in front of the old stone mansion and I took a deep breath.

"You can do this, Lorraine," Andy said, taking my hand. It was his idea to go visit my parents.

I nodded, got Alex from the back seat, and we all walked up to the front door. I took a deep breath, and rang the doorbell. Dorothea answered. She looked the same after 13 years.

"Can I help you?" she asked.

"Dorothea, it's me, Lorraine."

"Lorraine? Lorraine! You're so beautiful! And who is this?" she cried, looking at Alex.

"This is my daughter, Alex. This my son Joey, and this is my husband, Andy."

"It's nice to meet you, ma'am," Andy said, shaking Dorothea's hand.

"Come on, in, I'll call your mother."

We followed Dorothea inside and I saw that nothing had changed in 13 years. I took a deep breath and then I saw my mother walk into the foyer.

"Lorraine."

"Hello mother."

"I missed you so much!" she cried, giving me a hug. I couldn't help but let the tears stream down my face.

"I missed you too, mom. Where's dad?"

"Lorraine, there's something I need to tell you."

"What is it?"

"Y-your f-father i-is d-dead," she stammered.

"Oh my God," I gasped.

"He had a heart attack five years ago. T-there was nothing we could do to s-save him. I'm so sorry, sweetie."

"It's fine, mom. I'll be fine."

"So, who is this fox?" she asked, looking at Andy.

"Mom, this is my husband, Andy."

"It's very nice to meet you, Mrs. Cochrane," Andy said, shaking my mother's hand. She smiled at me.

"And who are you, fine sir?" she asked, kneeling down by Joey. He hid behind Andy's legs. Although he was nine years old, he was still a very shy kid.

"That's Joey, and this is Alexandra. Joey, say hello to your grandma."

"Hi, grandma," he mumbled.

"It's very nice to meet you, Joey. You've got your daddy's looks, don't you?"

Joey nodded.

"And Alexandra is as pretty as her momma was when she was little. How old is she?"

"Alexandra is almost three."

"You're getting big then, aren't you?"

Alexandra nodded.

"So, shall we have some dinner?" she suggested.

"That sounds good with me. What about you, Lorraine?"

"Dinner with my mom sounds amazing," I said.

"Well then, come on. Let's sit down before the food gets cold."

We had dinner, and talked about what I missed while in Magnolia. I felt the best I had in years. Suddenly, the phone rang. Dorothea picked it up.

"Andy, it's for you," she said, handing him the phone.

"Hello? No, you can't be serious. We're on our way," he gasped, hanging up the phone. He began to shake.

"Andy, what is it?" I asked, standing up.

"Lewis is dead."

And within 30 seconds, I felt like I was hit with a car. It's funny how things can change so quickly.

Part Two

Tales of a Teenage Piano Man

Chapter 1

Much Ado About Posters

I walked down the silent halls of Magnolia High School humming my favorite song, "(Just Like) Starting Over," by John Lennon to myself while hanging posters for the student showcase on the walls. That was when I heard muffled singing partnered with a string arrangement. That was also the moment my life changed forever.

I knew the song right away. It was "Yesterday" by The Beatles. I crept to the source of the sound, which was the auditorium, and snuck inside, undetected.

On the stage was a brown-haired, bespectacled girl playing the cello. Two blond-haired teens—a boy and girl—were playing violin, and a raven-haired girl was playing viola. And then I saw her. A girl, standing center stage and singing, had caught my attention. She had hair the color of fire that fell just past her shoulders and onto an old leather jacket covering a Billy Joel t-shirt. She also had on ripped jeans and old Chuck Taylors. You can tell a lot about a person from their sense of style, and I could tell we had a lot in common. As the song ended, I slowly began to walk towards the stage.

"Hey, you! Get out of here!" the blond-haired boy barked.

"Stand down. I come in peace," I said, putting my hands up. "I heard you in the hallway and I wanted to see the faces."

"What's your name?" the red-haired girl asked.

"I'm Joe, short for Joseph. And you are?"

"None of your business. Can't you see we're in the middle of rehearsal?"

"Oh, don't worry, I'm a fellow musician."

"Really? Why don't you show us what you got?" the raven-haired girl asked.

"Sure, you got a piano or guitar anywhere?"

"Dude, the piano's right over there," the brown-haired girl said, pointing behind the group. I jumped onto the stage and sat down at the piano.

"You need sheet music?"

"Nope," I said.

I began to play the melody at the beginning of "The Stranger" by Billy Joel. Towards the end of the song I also sang some of the lyrics.

When the song ended, the raven-haired girl asked, "How did you do that?"

"I have a photographic memory," I said, tapping the side of my head. "And by the way, 'The Stranger' is a better Billy Joel album than 'An Innocent Man.'"

I walked out of the auditorium nonchalantly and continued to hang posters. Suddenly, I heard footsteps behind me.

"You know, it wasn't nice to walk out like that."

It was the red-haired girl. She was standing in the center of the hallway with her arms crossed.

"Excuse me? I'm pretty sure your boyfriend wanted me out, so I left after I proved my musician status. It wasn't rude at all."

"Caleb's not my boyfriend. He just likes to think he is."

"Guess what? I don't really care," I said, walking down the

hallway. I didn't hear any footsteps, so I stopped hanging up posters and went into the music room.

I took out my electric guitar and plugged it into the amp. I began to play "While My Guitar Gently Weeps" by George Harrison. I have great respect for all of the Beatles, but George has always been my favorite.

When I finished that song, I switched to the piano and played "Crocodile Rock" by Elton John, enthusiastically singing along. When I came to the end of the song, I got up and walked to class. At the end of the day, I finished hanging up posters.

"I've seen you before, Joe," someone walked up to me and said.

"Oh, you have?" I asked sarcastically.

"Yeah. You're always studying sheet music, but this morning was the first time I'd seen you play anything."

"What? It's out of the ordinary for a musician to study sheet music?" I asked, turning to see the red-haired girl walking up to me.

"I don't appreciate sarcasm."

"Too bad, I'm a very sarcastic person," I said, walking off. I headed home on the warm October day and arrived just as my mom was pulling into the driveway.

"Hi, Joe. How was your day?" she asked, getting out of her car.

"Perfectly average. Nothing new happened. Nothing out of the ordinary," I said, walking inside. I entered my room and picked up the book we were reading in English class, which was *To Kill A Mockingbird* by Harper Lee. I read it the day we got it, but we have a test tomorrow, so I'd like to refresh my memory.

After a couple minutes, my fingers were itching for some piano keys to touch or a guitar chord to play so I sat down at the old piano in the corner of my room. I started to play

"Uptown Girl" by Billy Joel, then my nuisance of a little sister, Alex, came running into the room. Even though she stresses over the little things way too much, she's still the sweetest little girl I've ever met. She's also really smart.

"What's wrong now?" I asked.

"I failed a test!" my 11-year-old sister cried.

"That's it?"

"What do you mean 'that's it'! What if I don't get into college? What if I have to work at a call center?"

"Lex, you're in sixth grade. Colleges don't look at your grades until high school."

"So, you're the one in danger of not making it into college."

"Hey! I have straight-A's!"

"Ugh, you're too smart. It's no fun to tease you," she sighed, stomping out of my room.

"I love you too, sis!" I hollered.

"Can you play the song?" she asked, appearing in my room again.

"But of course." I said, grabbing my acoustic guitar. I played "Blackbird" by The Beatles and Lex sang along. Lex is a really good singer. She's the youngest member of our church choir.

When the song was over, Lex said, "Thank you Joe," and gave me a hug.

I love playing music, but playing it for Alex just makes me even happier. She never judges me. She just listens and sings along if she knows the words. Alex is a good kid. And very smart. She'll definitely get into an Ivy-League school like Harvard or Yale. I'm gonna be the one working in a call center.

I sat back on my bed and quietly strummed the chords from John Lennon's song, "Imagine."

Chapter 2

Starting Over

Music. The true pursuit of happiness. My true American dream. No matter what notes are played, they convey emotion.

That's what I love most about music. It doesn't matter what you sing or play, it's gonna strike a chord with somebody and they'll laugh or cry or smile, and that's when you know they remember something they associate with a song similar to it.

I started singing the words to Lennon's "(Just Like) Starting Over." When I had finished, I walked over to the piano and sat down on the bench. I stretched my fingers over the keys and began to play a familiar tune by Bill Withers. Lewis had played "Lean on Me" for me before my first piano lesson. I can remember every word he said.

"Now, son, I don't expect you to be able to play this at first, but with my help, you'll be the best piano player in Magnolia. This is my favorite song because it reminds me of your dad and the girl I loved in high school. I don't want you to ever forget this song. Let it stay with you until you see that white light. Joe, this is what the best music is," he had said.

I felt tears in my eyes as I remembered what Lewis had

said about the song I was now playing. I was jolted back to the present when I heard an angelic voice belt out, "We all need somebody to lean on."

I stopped playing and looked up to see the red-haired girl standing in the doorway of the music room. She was wearing a blue dress and the Chuck Taylors.

"What do *you* want?" I asked.

"I want you to play in my band."

"Ha! That's hilarious! You call an egotistical singer surrounded by a string quartet a band? Please, tell me that was a joke!"

"Um, excuse me, but when did we start talking about you?"

"Um, excuse me. Why don't you jump from your ego and down to your IQ?"

"I'm being completely serious right now!"

"So am I! Besides, I'm not gonna be some pawn for a singer to boss around. I work alone," I said, walking out of the music room.

"Excuse me? You're saying *I* have a big ego? You're the one acting like - I don't know, Madonna?"

"Hey! That's an insult and you know it!"

"Tell me, oh interesting one, why is that an insult?"

"Madonna's washed up! She had her 15 minutes of fame, but now she's been replaced. No one cares!" I shouted in the empty hall. I stormed off.

"My name's Estella, by the way!"

Later in the day after that encounter, I sat down in my English class and took out *To Kill A Mockingbird*. I read the last two pages and put it back in my bag before anyone else got in the room.

"Good morning, class! Who's ready for a test?" my English teacher, Mr. Greene, hollered, walking into the classroom. Everyone groaned.

Suddenly, there was a faint knock on the door.

"Good morning, Mr. Greene. My schedule got changed, and I was told I'm now in this hour," the red-haired girl muttered. I don't seem to remember her name. Maybe I am egotistical like she said.

"Yes, come in, Estella," he said.

"Thank you, Mr. Greene," she whispered, sitting down in the front row.

Mr. Greene handed out the tests, and I sped through it because every question was easy, not because I wanted to be the first one done. In fact, I checked my answers five times as I waited for someone to turn theirs in first. Once a girl who sat in the back row with me started walking back to her seat, I scribbled my name on my test and turned it in. I then sat at my desk and studied sheet music until everyone was done.

"Attention students! To end our unit on *To Kill A Mockingbird*, we will be starting a project based on the theme of one student in this class! Now, who would like to share the theme they came up with?" Mr. Greene asked. No one raised their hand. He looked directly at me and I slowly shook my head.

"No," I mouthed.

"Mr. Grayson! Why don't you tell us your theme!"

That girl turned to look at me and I took a deep breath.

"Differences are what bring people closer together," I mumbled, fiddling around with my pencil.

"Excuse me, Mr. Grayson, but could you speak a little louder?"

"Differences are what bring people closer together," I repeated, raising my voice level.

"Great theme, Mr. Grayson! What leads you to believe that?"

"Well, throughout the story, all of the characters are making assumptions about each other and highlighting each other's differences."

"Mr. Grayson, would you care to elaborate on that statement?" Mr. Greene asked, sitting on the edge of his desk.

"Well, everyone thinks that Boo Radley is this murderous psycho, but Scout doesn't want to exactly believe that, and she becomes friends with him in the end. She wanted to meet the guy before she made assumptions. And Atticus was constantly thought of as a lawyer, and a widower, and a father, but when he decided to defend Tom Robinson, the majority of the town turned on him, and a lot of people thought he wouldn't go through with the trial. And once he does go through with the trial, despite losing, everyone in town changes their opinions about him. And Tom Robinson is falsely accused of an offense by the Ewells because he's black," I said.

Mr. Greene stared at me, dumbfounded, until he slowly began to clap. The entire class joined in, and that girl smiled at me and I nearly melted. She seemed happy, albeit confused about what was going on. As the applause died down, a couple of kids in my class gave me high-fives and patted me on the back.

"Amazing interpretation, Joe! Now, for our project choices, you can interview someone and write a paper about them, make a movie, review the movie, do something with art, or perform a song, whether you wrote it or someone else did."

I already knew what I was gonna do. The choice was clear. Of course I would perform a song. Now I just had to pick a song.

Once class was over, I walked out before that girl could catch up to me. Sadly, it didn't work.

"Joe! Wait up!"

"What do you want?"

"Can I interview you for my project?"

"Depends. What do I get out of it?"

"I'll help you with your project!"

"That's a good start. I'll take that, but I need just a little bit more. I'm thinking of performing in the student showcase and I could use a female singer along with a guitarist. You think you could do it?"

"Sure!"

"Great. Now, what song do you think I should perform for the showcase?"

"Let me get back to you on that."

"Thank you-"

"Estella. Estella James."

"Thank you, Estella," I said, as I walked into math class.

"Wait, Joe!" said Estella, before I could take my seat.

"What?"

"Why was everyone applauding in class?"

"That was the first time I talked this year."

Chapter 3

Joe Grayson's Lonely Hearts Club Band

The next morning, I got up, got dressed, and walked to school. Estella drove up right as I was walking in. She was carrying a battered guitar case.

"Good morning!" she chirped.

"Yeah, sure," I said, unlocking the door to the music room. We walked in and I set everything up while Estella tuned her guitar and plugged it into the amp.

"So, I came up with two songs you could use for your project."

"Okay, what are they?"

"'Come Together' by The Beatles and 'Imagine' by John Lennon."

"Good choices. I think I'll go with 'Come Together.'"

"Sounds good. So, do you have any ideas for a set list?"

"Well, we get ten minutes for performances, so I was thinking you perform a song and I accompany you, and I play a song and you accompany me, and then we do a song together."

"That sounds like a fair plan. So, what song should we do together?"

"Well, we could do 'Everybody Wants to Rule the World' by Tears For Fears, 'Dancing in the Street' by David Bowie and Mick Jagger, 'Games People Play' by Joe South, 'Don't Go Breaking My Heart' by Elton John and Kiki Dee, or 'Help!' by The Beatles."

"I can't decide between 'Everybody Wants to Rule the World,' 'Games People Play,' and 'Don't Go Breaking My Heart.'"

"Then why don't we do that for our set list and we could do them all together?"

"Sounds good with me. Let's start practicing."

Estella took the lead on "Don't Go Breaking My Heart" for a short time while I worked on the chords for "Games People Play," and I couldn't help but smile when I heard her sing.

Chapter 4

The Ballad of Estella James

My name is Estella James, and I'm in love with Joe Grayson. I have been since I moved here in the sixth grade. There's just one problem. I have less than a year to live, so I'm not even gonna try.

I have an irregular heartbeat, and my doctors can't treat it. I think of every day I don't go without a heart attack as one less day until I actually do have one.

My doctors have said multiple times that the first heart attack I have will be my last one. That's how irregular my heartbeat is.

Anyway, so I just got closer to Joe, and it feels great. I just can't tell him about my heart. He can't distance himself from me.

We just finished rehearsal for the showcase, and now I'm in English class.

"Good morning, students! Today, we will be having a talent show of sorts! It will continue until we've gotten through everyone in the class! Who wants to go first?" Mr. Greene shouted. He was a very loud man, which seems like quite the accomplishment, because he's been here for about a thousand years. A large cluster of kids raised their hands. I was waiting until I was the second-to-last person, because I figured Joe would want to do the grand finale.

After watching multiple monologues from the theater geeks, a rehearsed game of catch from the jocks, and multiple attempts at singing, it was my turn.

"So, Miss James, what will you be delighting us with this morning?" Mr. Greene asked as I walked to the front of the classroom.

"I will be singing 'Help!' by The Beatles." I said.

"Good choice. Whenever you're ready."

"Help! I need somebody," I began.

Once the song was finished, I sat down, and Joe stood up, just like I guessed.

"Joe, you are our grand finale, I guess. What will you be singing?"

"'It's Still Rock n' Roll to Me' by Billy Joel."

"Great choice! Whenever you're ready."

"Just one more thing. We kind of have to move to the music room for my performance."

"Everybody! Get up, we're going for a field trip!" Mr. Greene shouted. Everyone got up and we began to run down the halls. When we got to the music room, Joe sat down at the piano and gestured for me to pick up my guitar and start playing.

We went back and forth, singing the lyrics, and eventually the entire class joined in. The bell rang just as we were finishing the song. After school, Joe and I rehearsed again, and then I went home.

Chapter 5

Jumping Is Hard to Do

It has been about a week since the "talent show" in English class, and nothing has changed. Estella and I have been rehearsing three times a day for the showcase.

"Estella?" I asked, stopping rehearsal.

"What?"

"Are sure you want to perform at the showcase?"

"Of course I do," she said. "Don't you?"

"Yeah, I guess," I shrugged.

"Then we're gonna do this! Now, if you'll excuse me, I have to go talk to Mr. Greene about my project," she said, walking out of the music room.

Later that morning when the time for English class came, it began with Mr Greene saying, "Good, morning, class! Today, we will be dipping our feet into adventure! Follow me, we have a little field trip to embark on."

Everyone got up and Mr. Greene led the class out into the hallway. After walking all the way across the school, he finally stopped at the gym doors. "Students, welcome to your adventure," he said, opening the gym doors to reveal a giant trampoline and a platform.

"Mr. Greene, what does this have to do with adventure?" Tara, the smartest girl in class asked, raising her hand.

"We will be jumping from that platform onto the trampoline while shouting out our greatest fears."

"Mr. Greene, are you sure that's safe?" she asked.

"Don't worry, the principal approved it, and we've taken all the proper safety precautions. Now, let's jump!" he said, leading us into the gym. I took a deep breath. My greatest fear is heights.

Once we were on the platform, Mr. Greene called everyone up by name.

"Hey, if you don't want to do this, I bet Mr. Greene would let you sit out," I whispered.

"Funny, I was just about to say that to you. Scared yet, Grayson?"

"Sorry for being afraid of heights," I gulped, looking at the gym floor. "That's an awful long way down."

"Estella! You're up!"

"I'm coming!" she shouted, parting the crowd. I forced my way through behind her. She walked to the edge of the platform and I closed my eyes.

"Estella, what is your greatest fear?"

"Having a life devoid of adventure!"

"Great! Now, jump!"

I looked down at my feet. I didn't want to see if she made it or not.

"Mr. Greene, is there any way I can jump with Joe? Just so he's not alone?" she asked. I looked up and saw Mr. Greene nodding.

"Joe, get over here," he said.

"I didn't want you to be too scared," she whispered.

"Joe, what is your greatest fear?"

"Heights!"

"And you're sure you're actually going to jump?"

"Lean on me, when you're not strong," Estella sang under her breath. I took her hand. I gulped. We were really high up. I studied the trampoline. There was still the possibility of it breaking. I looked at Estella's pale hands. This was just an irrational fear, right? What if it meant something more?

"What if it meant something more?" I asked myself.

"Did you say something, Joe?" she asked.

"Let's do this," I murmured.

"What?"

"Let's do this! Let's jump!" I cried, hopping off the platform. It was in that moment that I knew what I had to do.

I have to tell Estella how I feel.

Chapter 6

The Ballad of Estella James Continues

I have to tell Joe how I feel.

The clock is ticking. I need to tell him before I'm gone. That jump today justified everything.

"I'm ready for my interview," he said, walking into the music room after school. I was sitting at the piano.

"Okay, well, I guess I'm the interviewer, so, just sit down right there," I said, pointing to a chair next to the piano bench.

"So, what's my first question?" he asked, sitting down.

"We'll ease into it. What's your favorite color?"

"Green."

"What's your favorite book and why?"

"My favorite book *is The Catcher in the Rye* because I feel like I can relate to Holden in a way."

"Okay, now we're digging a little deeper. What is one secret you're willing to share with me?"

"I missed my sixth birthday."

"How did you miss your sixth birthday?"

"Oh, you'll find out soon."

"Okay then. I'm digging a little bit deeper. Who is one person who changed your life the most?"

"My piano teacher Lewis. He was my dad's best friend from the age of eight to 35 years old."

"How come they're not friends anymore?"

"Lewis died when I was nine. We were visiting my grandma in East Hampton when my dad got a call saying that he had been murdered. His wife disappeared with his killer. No one can find either of them. Remember when I was singing 'Lean On Me' in here and you sang a verse?"

"Yeah," I nodded, unable to say much more.

"That was the first song Lewis played for me right before he taught me to play piano. Before he played the song, he said to me: 'Now, son, I don't expect you to be able to play this at first, but with my help, you'll be the best piano player in Magnolia. This is my favorite song because it reminds me of your dad and the girl I loved in high school. I don't want you to ever forget this song. Let it stay with you until you see that white light. Joe, this what the best music is.'"

"I'm so sorry, Joe."

"It's fine, really," he shrugged.

"If you say so. Next question it is. What is one thing I don't know about you?" I asked. He took a deep breath.

"I'm the kid who was kidnapped by his uncle in 1982. That's how I missed my sixth birthday."

"Oh my God. How did you recover from that?"

"A lot of nightmares and therapy, along with a loving family. Is it okay if we cut this short? I have to get home."

"Yeah, there's just one more question. What's your favorite song?"

"'Yesterday' by The Beatles," he said, walking out of the room. I sat down at the piano and began playing Bonnie Tyler's "Total Eclipse of the Heart."

Chapter 7

Turnaround

I've realized my problem. I'm too analytical. I overthink things more than I need to. Sure, that's good in some situations, but it's the worst in others.

One example is if you're in love with Estella James, the girl who doesn't believe in second thoughts or cold feet.

When I'm with Estella, I know that all of the overthinking I've ever done is useless.

Estella doesn't think. She just acts. I don't know why, but that's why I love her.

"Joseph Lloyd Grayson! Get down here! You're gonna be late for school!" my mom shouted from downstairs.

"I'm coming!" I hollered, grabbing my acoustic guitar. I sprinted down the stairs, nearly tripping over Alex's cat, Trixie.

"Come on, Joe, I'll give you a ride to school," my dad said, getting up from the kitchen table.

"Bye, Joe," Alex said, digging into a bowl of cereal. I walked out of my house and climbed into my dad's truck.

"So, how's school?"

"It has always been the same. Nothing new."

"How is practice for the showcase going?"

"It's going well."

"Bye, Joe."

"Bye, Dad."

I ran inside and took my seat right as the bell rang.

"Welcome to presentation day! Since Joe was almost late, I suggest we have him go first! Joe, do you have anything to say about that?"

"Nope," I said, taking my guitar out of the case.

"And what will you be delighting us with today?" Mr. Greene asked, sitting down at his desk.

"I will be performing an acoustic version of 'Under Pressure' by David Bowie and Queen."

"Whenever you're ready."

I slung my guitar onto my shoulder and began to play. When I reached the end, I tried my best to finish strong. When I finished, I was greeted by an avalanche of applause from my classmates. I had improved a lot this year.

"Thank you very much," I said, taking a bow. I sat down at my desk and put my guitar back in the case.

A few more students did their presentations after I took my seat. I was daydreaming when Mr. Green came up to me and said, "Joe, can I talk to you for a second?"

Chapter 8

The Ballad of Estella James Ends

We just had presentations of our projects in English, and now I'm just playing random stuff in the music room. I began to sing "What I Did for Love," my favorite song from "A Chorus Line."

I had barely gotten through the first stanza when I stopped as my breath became short and labored. I felt a pain in my left arm. This was happening. This was my ending. I opened my mouth to scream, but no sound came out. As rain hammered the windows, I fell to the floor, unable to move.

I thought of Joe, and how heartbroken he would be when he found out. I don't think I would ever recover if he died.

I've never enjoyed the ending of anything. Especially when I really enjoyed something, or it felt like it should have been longer. I heard shouts, but I couldn't decipher them. I felt the presence of people, but I couldn't acknowledge them. This was what it felt like to be dead. I'm dead. This is what it feels like. Suddenly, I saw a white light. I walked towards it and met a man by the name of Lewis. He introduced me to some people, and he showed me where I could see Joe. I didn't want to see what he was like at the moment, but I forced myself to watch.

He was running away. Joe was running away. He caught a Greyhound bus and left Magnolia. He got a job at some jazz club, playing piano, and he met a girl. They fell in love. They got married.

He didn't love me. He never loved me. I was just his friend, Estella. I was just his singing partner. I just allowed him to have extra piano practice. When I saw this series of images, I couldn't help but feel like I was hit with a ton of bricks.

"He never loved me," I whispered under my breath. No one heard. No one cared. I should've gone out with Caleb when I had the chance. Maybe then I wouldn't have died alone.

I died alone because Joe didn't love me.

Chapter 9

Kiss Today Goodbye

"Is everything okay, Mr. Greene?" I asked, walking up to his desk.

"You need to tell Estella how you feel sooner rather than later," he said, point-blank. I hesitated.

"What are you talking about?"

"Give it a rest, Joe, I see the way you look at her, and I heard her sing to you before you said something to yourself during the jumping exercise. It's not hard to see. I know she's the one that should be telling you this, but she's dying from an irregular heartbeat. Her doctors can't treat it. Her parents told me the first heart attack she has will be her last."

"Why didn't she tell me?"

"She was probably waiting for the right moment. Don't worry about it. Her doctors are saying she won't be gone in an hour or anything like that, although it is a risk," Mr. Greene asked.

"It's a risk? I need to find her! Do you know where she is?"

"I think I saw her walking down the music hallway."

"Thank you, Mr. Greene!" I shouted, sprinting down the hallway. When I got to the music room, I took a deep breath, trying to collect my thoughts, when I heard a thud. I opened the door to see Estella on the floor, not moving.

"Somebody call an ambulance!" I cried, collapsing in the doorway. Rain pounded against the windows as a fleet of teachers and paramedics tried to revive her. There was no hope.

Estella died from a heart attack. Two months later, I performed alone at the showcase. I played "Lean On Me" by Bill Withers, "Imagine" by John Lennon, "Yesterday" by The Beatles, and "She's Got A Way" by Billy Joel.

"Joe, here's your mail," my mom said three days after the showcase. I've been a shell of a person. She set my mail on my bed and I glanced at it. The top envelope had Estella's handwriting.

"Impossible," I whispered, lifting up the envelope. I opened it and began to read.

> *Dear Joe,*
>
> *If you're reading this, it means I'm gone. I'm sorry I never told you about my condition, and I'm sorry this letter wasn't sent earlier. I wanted to give you time to adjust to being without me. I love you, Joe, and I hope you love me, too, even if it is just as a friend.*
>
> *– Estella*
>
> *P.S., I hear New York is nice in the Fall."*

I felt tears in my eyes and didn't stop them from falling. I got up and grabbed all of the money I earned from mowing lawns, $4,000 that I never spent. I was going to put it towards college, but I now had another idea. I'm gonna drop out of high school and go to New York, just like Lewis did, except I'm gonna make it big. I'm gonna be famous.

Two weeks later, I packed a suitcase, grabbed my money, and hopped on a Greyhound bus and rode to New York City.

When I got there, I immediately started singing the words

to the song, "New York, New York" as I walked down the crowded streets, clutching the old journal Lewis kept when he was in high school. Mr. Greene gave it to me when I told him I was leaving for New York. This was my new home. I was never going back to Magnolia. That town might as well not exist in my world.

Chapter 10

New York, New York

After three days of staying in the cheapest hotel in New York— which was still expensive—I found a jazz club looking for a piano player. It was also relatively close to the record labels, so it was in a prime location. I walked in and gave my resume to the manager, and old man named William.

"Well, you've had no job experience other than mowing lawns for eight years, but you have been playing the piano for eleven years and you have a photographic memory, which could help with entertainment value, because I figure a young kid like you is looking for anything. Can you play something for me?" William asked.

"Sure," I said, walking onto the stage. "Is there anything you'd want me to play?" I asked.

"Play the prelude and 'Angry Young Man' from Billy Joel's *Turnstiles* album. If you're up for it that is."

"Please, I learned how to play that song six years ago," I shrugged.

"Then play it. Don't act like you can play it, actually play it."

"Okay," I said, then cracked my knuckles and began to play. I sang the song too. When I had finished, William said, "My God, you're the best pianist I've had apply! Why aren't you at a record label right now?"

"You mean none of the people who have applied have been able to play this? Did any of them have experience in modern music? I began piano with a Billy Joel song!"

"Son, I like your ambition and drive. You're hired," William said, shaking my hand.

Chapter 11

My Life As A Big Shot

I've been playing at that jazz club for six years now. I obviously haven't been discovered yet.

"Good luck tonight, Joe! I bet those suits will love you!" my girlfriend and co-worker Sadie said. She's a waitress at the club. There's an open mic night down the street and there's a rumor that some suits from a big record label are gonna be there to recruit some new talent.

"Welcome to open mic night! I'm Danny Edmond, your host for the night!"

Danny Edmond owns a club that holds Amateur Hour every Friday, but we had to sign up in advance for tonight. Danny's my best friend and neighbor.

"What'll you have tonight, Joe?" his wife, Charlotte asked.

"I'll have a beer, Charlotte," I said, sitting down at the bar.

"Coming right up, Joe. You nervous?"

"Just a little bit," I said, looking up to see a band playing "Everybody Have Fun Tonight" by Wang Chung. They were doing okay, but not good enough. They weren't getting picked up. A few more okay people played. They weren't getting picked up either.

"Okay! Up next is my close friend, Joe Grayson!" Danny announced. I walked onto the stage.

"Good evening, everybody! I'm Joe Grayson, and tonight I will be playing 'American Pie' by Don McLean."

"Give it up for Joe Grayson!" Danny shouted, running off the stage. I sat down at the piano. I sang and played the entire song, and I think I did okay. That's kind of a hard song for me because Estella and I used to play it when we were tired of playing the same three songs during every rehearsal.

Once everyone had finished, I got up to leave, thinking I wasn't going to get picked up, but then I heard footsteps behind me.

"You're Joe Grayson, right?" one of the suits asked.

"Yeah," I said, stopping in the middle of the empty sidewalk.

"I'm Edward Robbins and this is Paul Johnson. We're executives at Atlantic Records. We want you to come in and play for our boss tonight. Can you do that?"

"Of course I can do that," I said as a limo pulled up to the curb. We climbed in and I rode to Atlantic Records.

"Sir, we have the kid," Mr. Johnson said, leading me into an office with a baby grand piano in the center.

"Great. Sit down at the piano, play me something," a man said. He was sitting in a chair turned away from us. I sat down at the piano and began to play Billy Joel's "Vienna."

I had only made it through the first three verses when a man barked, "Stop!"

I took my hands off the keys and put my hands in my lap. Mr. Robbins and Mr. Johnson shrugged. "Your name's Joseph Grayson, right?" the man asked.

"Yes, sir," I nodded.

"Welcome to Atlantic Records, Joseph Grayson," he said. "Now, if you'll excuse me, I have work to do. Be here tomorrow morning at 8:30."

That next morning, I got a record deal and made it big. Sadie and I got married that fall, and we had a son, who I named Lewis.

Two years after Lewis was born, Sadie left me to pursue
a career in acting, and I spent my life devoted to my son
and my music. As Lewis grew older, he became better at the
piano than me, just like what happened with his namesake.
I spent my entire life trying to embody what real music was,
but I was never as good as the man who taught me.

Part Three

Thank You For the Music

Chapter 1

Prelude

My name is Lewis William Ebbs, and I'm a ghost. I died on a cool September day in 1985. I left behind quite the legacy.

Ever since I was young, I had wanted to be the greatest piano player to ever live. That didn't exactly happen though because my best friend's nine-year-old son was better than me.

I bet you're wondering how I died. I got shot trying to save an innocent life. That's all I'll tell you for now.

I was born in Harlem, New York, during the middle of my dad's attempt to launch a career in jazz music. My parents had four more kids, all girls, before they decided to relocate to Magnolia, West Virginia, where we were the only black family. At first, it was hard, but with help from my best friend, Andy Grayson, whose dad was a distinguished member of the community, my family was accepted into daily life. I was even the Valedictorian at my high school graduation.

Even though I felt so different compared to everyone else, I knew that they would always accept me. I always hoped that my kids would get to see the acceptance Magnolia gave me instead of the hate going on around the rest of the country.

I never had the chance to have children. My wife and I never even talked about kids. We both wanted a big family, and if we had met earlier, maybe that would've happened.

Now I'm just some ghost. I can't be at peace until they find the person who killed me. That's what needs to happen. Someone needs to find my killer. Someone needs to find the man who almost killed my wife.

He had blond hair, yellow eyes, and scars across the right side of his face. He was wearing the kind of uniform one wears in prison. The man is a criminal, and he needs to be put in a maximum security prison like Alcatraz, even though it's not in use anymore.

Because of that man, I will never be at peace. Because of that man, I will always be Lewis William Ebbs, the ghost. It's not fun being a ghost.

Chapter 2

An Introduction to My Family

I n the 1920s, my grandfather packed a single suitcase, grabbed his old beat-up trumpet, and left the town closest to Magnolia. He was headed to Harlem to be a big jazz star, but he fell in love instead.

Her name was Jean, and her singing act came before his jazz band at a club. She had dark hair and big eyes, real big eyes. They got married after a month and became a jazz duo. One year later, they gave birth to a boy, who they named Leonard, or Lenny, my dad. Along with my grandparents, my dad grew up in Harlem and around music. He soon became a band director for a fancy hotel for the elderly. One Winter, he met the newest maid, Alessandra. The two of them got married in the Summer of 1953, and soon had a son named Lewis, a.k.a, me. They had four more kids, all girls born a year apart. Their names were Sally, Laurie, Irene, and Jane. After Alessandra gave birth to Jane, Lenny moved everyone back down to West Virginia - including my grandparents. That was the summer I met a young fellow by the name of Andrew Grayson. The year was 1962, and we were nine-years-old.

"Lewis! Where'd you run off to?" my mother asked as I stood on the lawn looking at the playground full of white boys and girls. I wasn't allowed to go and join them.

"He's right here, Andra!" my dad shouted, walking across the dead grass towards me. My mom followed after him, my newborn sister Jane in her arms.

"Lewis, why don't you go play with those kids? You could make some friends."

"I can't, Ma," I said, not looking away from the horrible sign. It was the sign that kept me from making friends in Harlem.

"Why not, Lewis? You're good at making friends," my pa said, kneeling next to me in the dead grass.

"Sign," I said, pointing to the bulletin in front of the playground.

"'Whites Only,' Come on, Lewis, let's get you inside," my ma sighed, taking my hand. I walked through the chaotic house to my bedroom. I closed the door and heard shouts erupt from the kitchen.

"What were you thinking, Lenny? None of our kids are gonna be able to make friends!" my ma cried.

"The same thing would've happened back in Harlem! Segregation is everywhere!"

"You're right, but that's not what I'm talking about! We're the only black family in this dead-end town! Where are we supposed to go to run errands? They're not gonna build a whole grocery store for a family of eight!"

"There'll be more families coming here."

"What about your work? I doubt the white men in the town band will want a black man leading them!" my ma shouted as I crept into the kitchen.

"Maybe if my father had never-"

"Don't pull your father into this! Larry had a dream, and he dropped everything to pursue it!"

"Lewis, how long have you been there?" my father asked, his tone softening.

"It doesn't matter. Lenny, I'm going to unpack. We'll be talking about this later," my ma said, walking down the hallway. My father walked towards the refrigerator as I heard a knock on the door.

"Lewis, can you get that?" my father asked, leaning into the fridge. I nodded and walked to the front door. I opened it to see a little white boy, his arm poised to knock again.

"Good afternoon. I'm Andy Grayson. I'm your new neighbor. What's your name?"

"Huh?" I asked.

"I'm Andy," he said, his arm still outstretched.

"Dude, you okay? What's with your arm?" I asked.

"Oh, sorry. My Pa taught me to be prepared to shake the hand of anyone I meet, he said, lowering his arm.

"I'm Lewis Ebbs."

"It's a pleasure to make your acquaintance Lewis Ebbs," he said, shaking my hand a little too enthusiastically.

"Do you want to come inside?" I asked.

"Well, my Ma says not to talk to strangers, and my Pa says not to go into a stranger's house, so I'm not sure what to say," he shrugged.

"How about we just talk on the steps?" I suggested.

"That sounds fine," Andy nodded.

"You can wait here. I'll be right back," I said, walking into my house. I grabbed two bottles of cherry soda from the fridge.

"Lewis, who's at the door?" my pa asked, combing through a stack of magazines.

"My new friend, Andy. I'll be on the steps," I shrugged, walking back outside. I handed Andy a bottle and he looked at it quizzically. "Here, I can help you with that," I said, hitting the bottle on the brick flower boxes. I then twisted the cap and it came of easily. I did the same with mine and took a big swig of soda.

"What?" I asked, looking at Andy.

"How did you do that?"

"We used to do that all the time in Harlem. It was an easy way to open a bottle without breaking it."

"How do you remember that after all this time? Aren't teenagers the ones who usually do that?"

"Well, I also have this thing where I can remember almost anything I hear or see," I shrugged.

"A photographic memory?"

"Yeah, that's it!"

"I have a photographic memory too! My Ma says it's what makes me special and different from the other kids."

"No way! I thought I was the only one who had it! My parents told me to hide it and everything!"

"They probably don't want you to be too different. That's what my Ma and Pa also say," Andy shrugged.

"Yeah, I guess. What are your folks like?"

"They're okay. My Ma stays home with me and my brother Walt. My Pa's a detective at the police station. I want to do that when I get older. What about you?"

"I'm gonna be a jazz pianist. I can't play trumpet like my grandpa can, and I'm not a natural leader like my Pa."

"I can understand that. Lewis?"

"Yeah? I asked, looking away from the playground.

"You wanna be friends?"

"Best friends," I said, shaking Andy's hand. We spent the rest of the afternoon talking about whatever we wanted.

"Andy, can I ask you a question?"

"Sure you can."

"Why do you wanna be friends with me? Wouldn't your parents get mad?"

"My parents hate these dumb Jim Crow laws. They think

everyone should be treated the same, no matter what's different about them."

"But why me? Why did you want to be friends with me?"

"Because I think everyone needs a friend. Friends are the best gift a person could get. They listen to you, and help you up when you fall. Correct me if I'm wrong, but friends are for life."

"Andy promise me one thing."

"Of course."

"Through this friendship, we have to stop each other from doing stupid things."

"It's a promise," Andy said, giving me a high-five.

"Andrew Clarence Grayson! If you don't get in here right now, I'm throwing your dinner in the garbage!" Andy's mom shouted from a few houses down.

"See you tomorrow, Lewis!" Andy hollered, running across the dead grass to his house. I waved to him and walked inside.

Chapter 3

Magnolia Elementary

Two months later, no black families had moved to town, and we were still the outsiders. Today is my first day of the fourth grade at Magnolia Elementary. "Lewis! Andy's here!" my ma shouted.

"I'm coming, ma!" I hollered, putting my shoes on. I walked out into the kitchen and grabbed my backpack.

"Bye, Mrs. Ebbs!"

"Goodbye, Andy! Take good care of Lewis!"

Andy and I walked to school without getting strange looks from any of the townspeople. They were probably all at the school. As Andy and I walked up the stairs to the school doors, it was clear that I was right.

"Just stick with me, Lewis," Andy whispered as we slowly walked down the hallway. The hubbub of school starting had settled and an eerie silence had overcome the crowds. We turned towards the office and found out that we were in the same class.

When we got back out in the hallway, it was still silent. We walked to our classroom, Mrs. Jackson's classroom. We sat down in the back row, right next to each other. When the bell rang, students streamed into the classroom and the desk in front of me stayed empty.

"Good morning, class! Welcome to the fourth grade!" Mrs. Jackson chirped, walking into the classroom. "I am happy to announce that we have a new student with us this year! Everybody, please welcome Lewis!"

No one said hello. No one waved to me. Andy looked around, exasperated. I shook my head, trying to get him to sit down.

"Hey! This is my best friend, and he deserves some respect, even if he does have a different skin color! He's still a person!" Andy cried, standing up. Everyone in town knew not to mess with Andy's family. His dad was a powerful detective, and his mom was a very standoffish person, a woman everyone knew not to mess with.

Almost immediately, all of the kids began to wave and say hello to me. Although I was welcomed, it didn't feel right. For the rest of the day, no one talked to me except Andy and Mrs. Jackson. Andy and I then walked home and did our homework.

"I'm sorry about everyone. They're not exactly used to people, well, people like you," Andy muttered.

"Black people? I can tell, Andy. It's fine to call me black."

"Okay. I hope it gets better for you."

"I hope it gets better too."

Chapter 4

Mrs. Grayson

One thing I have learned from life is that we all experience life and death, whether it be the birth of a child, the death of a friend or family member, our own lives, or our death. I'll always remember five experiences with death I had. The first was Andy's mother, when we were both ten years old.

It was a cool winter morning in 1963 when we got the call. Andy's mom had died in her sleep the night before in the hospital. She had breast cancer.

"What am I gonna do without her, Lewis? She was my Ma," Andy whispered. We were sitting on the front porch.

"I dunno, Andy. Your Ma was such a great lady."

"She really was. How could one woman do so much when she was so sick?" Andy asked.

"Your Ma was a superhero. Just like Wonder Woman."

"Andy! Come on! We have to get to the funeral home!" Mr. Grayson barked. Andy shrugged and ran across the lawn, brushing off his suit. His father wanted her funeral to be as soon as possible.

I stood up and walked inside. We had to get ready for the funeral. After about 20 minutes, my family flocked out to our van and drove to the funeral home. When we arrived we walked inside and sat down in the front row, as Mr. Grayson had requested.

"Hey! People like *you* belong in the back!" a man growled as he sat down in the third row.

"Emmett! These people are family, and it was my request that they sit in the front row! Have a little decency, my wife *died* this morning," Mr. Grayson cried, facing the man. My ma patted his shoulder sympathetically as the tears streamed down his face. Slowly, the entire town streamed into the little chapel, and the service began.

"Citizens of Magnolia, we are gathered here to honor the life of Elaine Grayson. Many of us lost someone today. We lost a neighbor, a friend, a mother, and a wife. Now, could Mr. Lawrence Ebbs and his son, Lewis, please come to the piano? Mr. Grayson wanted you to play something for Elaine, because she enjoyed your piano playing so much," the town pastor said solemnly.

My pa and I sat down at the piano and began to play "My Prayer" by The Platters. When the song was over no one applauded, but I didn't care, because this day wasn't about us. This situation wasn't ours to try to get over.

At the end of the service, everyone rose and walked to the center of town for a vigil. There was a memorial at Magnolia Elementary, where Andy's mother helped out so often.

Chapter 5

Moving On Up

It has been four years since Mrs. Grayson passed away. Andy and I are in our first year of Magnolia High School, and I am finally feeling like a part of the community. In fact, I have become one of the most popular kids in my class. The year is 1967. It is the year I will meet the girl I want to spend the rest of my life with.

"Lewis! Wake up, it's time for school!" my ma shouted from the kitchen. I got up, got dressed, and walked out to the kitchen. I looked down at my ma and smiled.

My ma is very short. She's only five-foot-three, and I'm six-foot-one at just fourteen-years-old. I definitely have my pa's height.

"You have a good first day of school, son," she said, giving me a hug.

"Bye, Ma!" I said, walking out of the house. I met Andy at his driveway and we biked to school. We're in the ninth grade now, and two more black families have moved to the community. No one has met either of them yet because they live a long way outside of town. Andy and I are hoping to become friends with them today.

We locked our bikes and walked inside.

"Well, if it ain't Lewis! Hey everybody! Lewis's back from

Harlem!" Andy's cousin, Billy, announced. I went to Harlem with my dad over the summer to learn about the music he grew up with. We just got back last night. Let's just say I've gotten a lot better at playing piano and singing.

"Lewis! Welcome back, bud! Can you play something for us?" my other best friend, Marshall, asked.

"Sure, but I'm gonna need a piano," I shrugged. Everyone began to laugh. We flocked to the music room.

"So, what's it gonna be?"

"'Wonderful World' by Sam Cooke," I announced, sitting down at the piano. I began to play the chords. When I had finished, everyone applauded. I stood up and saw a girl standing in the door. She was smiling at me. I waved her in here, but she just sheepishly walked away.

She was black. That girl was from one of the new families. She was beautiful. More beautiful than any girl I'd ever seen.

"Come on, Lewis, it's time for class," Andy said, leading me off to class. We sat down in the back row, out of habit, and waited for class to start. We were all messing around and learning about each other's summers when that girl came into the classroom. We all stopped as she walked towards my desk.

"Is this seat taken?" she asked, pointing to the desk in front of me.

"N-no, feel free to sit there," I mumbled, shaking my head and sitting up. I looked over at Andy and he began to laugh.

"I'm Alexandra. I'm new to town," she said, turning around to face me. She was wearing a light yellow dress. The color suited her.

"It's nice to meet you, Alexandra, I'm Lewis."

"Good morning, class! Welcome to your first day of high school!" our homeroom teacher, Mr. Greene shouted, walking into the room. He was new this year. Mrs. Renson had retired. He was tall with blond hair and glasses. He was pushing a cart full of books.

"My name is Mr. Greene, and these are your journals for the next four years, as that is how long I will be your homeroom teacher! Please pass these back, and make sure not to lose them!"

The notebooks got passed down to Andy and I, and we looked at each other quizzically.

"Now, for your first entry tonight, I would like you to write about what you did this summer, what you like, who's in your family, stuff like that! Every night, you will have a journal assignment, and on Friday, you will hand your notebooks in and I will grade them! Now, let's get past that! I am also the new English teacher, as many of you know, and this is my first year teaching. I hope you make my first year as memorable as possible! So, today, I will do my best to learn your names! You, in the back!" he barked, pointing at me.

"Yes, Mr. Greene?"

"Stand up," he said. So, I stood. "What is your full name?"

"Lewis William Ebbs."

"It's nice to meet you, Lewis William Ebbs. What is something interesting you did over the summer?"

"I went to Harlem with my dad and he taught me what real music is."

"And what does he describe real music to be?"

"Jazz and soul, sir. He's the leader of the town band, and he taught me how to play piano."

"Very interesting. Can you play something for us?"

"Well, yeah, but I need a piano."

"It's right in that corner," he said, pointing to the corner behind me.

"If anybody wants to, feel free to join in."

"And what song will you be playing?" Mr. Greene asked.

"'Stand By Me' by Ben E. King, sir," I said, sitting down at the piano.

"Good choice. Go whenever you're ready."

I stretched my fingers over the keys and Andy and Billy read my mind. Andy grabbed an acoustic guitar from the cabinet and Billy found a sand shaking instrument. Then I began singing, "When the night has come."

When I got to the chorus, Alexandra stood up and sang out, "Stand by me." We sang the final verse together and when we were done everyone applauded. I smiled at Alexandra, then the bell rang. I walked out of Mr. Greene's room and walked to the American History classroom. Everyone proceeded with the rest of the day, and when the final bell rang, everyone flocked outside.

"Lewis! We're over here!" Andy shouted, waving from the end of the sidewalk. I ran over to my friends and I unlocked my bike.

"So, how was everybody's first day?" I asked as we biked down the street.

"That's what we should be asking *you*. Dude, you couldn't take your eyes off that new girl in our homeroom!" Billy exclaimed. We parked our bikes at the malt shop and sat down at a table. A flock of girls came in as we ordered a pizza and sat down at the booth behind us. Alexandra waved to me and I nervously waved back. She sat down with the girls.

"Okay boys, step aside, it's time for the old Grayson looks," Andy said, standing up. He walked over the booth and we heard him use one of his old pickup lines on the girls. Believe it or not, Andy was quite the ladies' man in high school.

"Good afternoon, ladies, sorry about not saving you sooner. I'm Lewis and ignore Andy. He just can't help but talk to all you beautiful girls. Come on, Andy, let's get you home," I sighed, turning Andy away from the girls. They all laughed.

"Dude, why'd you do that?" he asked as we unlocked our bikes.

"Because you would've embarrassed yourself like you always do. Come on, let's go home. We have to get this stupid journaling done for Mr. Greene."

So, Andy and I biked home, and instead of doing home-work like we should've been doing, we jammed out in my basement instead. I did my homework later that night.

It also turns out that I'm a pretty solid writer. I mean, writing well is pretty hard, but I feel like I'm a pretty solid writer. At least by high school standards.

The next day, I was in Mr. Greene's English class when something pretty weird happened.

"Good morning, class! Welcome to day two of high school! Will and John, will you please pass these books out?" Mr. Greene asked, pulling a cart of books in front of him.

"Sir? Isn't *The Catcher in the Rye* banned by the school district?" Alexandra asked, raising her hand.

"It is, but I think you should read this book because it could teach you a lot about the way you act around others," Mr. Greene said. "Now, who can tell me when this book was written?"

"Dude, Mr. Greene is pushing it. What do you wanna bet he's out by the end of the year?" Andy asked.

"I dunno," I shrugged.

"How about this. If Mr. Greene gets the boot by the end of next year, you have to ask that girl out," Andy said, pointing to Alexandra.

"Fine," I sighed.

"And it's a deal!"

Chapter 6

Small Town

Well, that's exactly what happened. Two years after that bet was made between Andy and I, Mr. Greene got the boot because the superintendent found out that he was teaching his students with banned books. Today's the first day of eleventh grade, and I have to ask Alex out by the end of the day.

"Good morning, old Lewis! Today's the day! How are you gonna do it?" Andy chirped, bursting into my room.

"Dude, who let you in?" I asked, sitting up.

"Your Pa. He was on his way to work. Well, how are you gonna ask her out?"

"I don't know, okay? Take a breather, Andy."

"Do you need any help?" he asked as I started getting dressed.

"From you? Heck no," I whispered, buttoning my shirt. "Dude, you have fewer moves than an old man about to lose a game of chess."

"Wow, brutal. That's new. So, you gonna serenade her or just ask her?"

"I don't know! Now, come on, let's get to school," I said, grabbing my backpack. We walked down the street and headed to Magnolia High School.

"So, got any ideas yet?" Andy asked as I sat down at the piano in the music room. I rolled my eyes.

"Will you just shut up already? She might hear you!"

"You're no fun. So, what Beatles song are we gonna play today? You have lost all appreciation for Jazz as it is."

"Today we will be playing 'All You Need Is Love' and I haven't lost *all* appreciation for Jazz music."

"Dude, couldn't you pick a newer Beatles song? We've been playing that since we were 10 years old!"

"We're doing an acoustic version this time. Totally different."

"Fine, let's get it over with," Andy sighed.

"Wait one second," I said, running out of the room. I scanned the hallways and found Alex sitting on the windowsill and reading.

"Hey Lewis, how was your summer?"

"I'll tell you later. Come on, I have a surprise for you," I said, leading her down the hallway. I sat her down in the music room and began playing the Beatles song, "All You Need is Love."

When I had finished she shouted, "That was amazing, Lewis!"

"Thank you. Andy, that was all I needed you for," I said, dismissing him and walking towards Alex.

"Bye bud, see you in homeroom," he said, winking at me.

"Alex, you're a really great girl."

"Thanks. You're pretty great too."

"Do you maybe want to go out to dinner sometime?"

"Lewis, I'd love to go on a date with you."

"Yes!" I cheered, giving her a hug as the bell rang. We ran off to homeroom, hand in hand.

When we walked into the English classroom, everybody went silent. I'm guessing Andy told them.

"She said yes!" I cried. Everybody cheered.

"Good morning, class! I'm glad to see my old homeroom

students! How was everyone's summer break?" Mr. Greene asked, walking into the classroom. Everyone gasped. "What? Surprised to see me? That's right, I didn't get fired!"

"But sir, didn't you appear in front of the superintendent and he sacked you?" Andy asked.

"Andy Grayson! For a detective's son, you aren't much good at taking notice of clues! The district superintendent is my brother! We were merely catching up with each other! Now, how was everyone's summer break? The suspense is killing me."

The rest of the day went by, and with that, the rest of the week, and then it was finally Saturday night, the night of my first date with Alex.

"Okay, Pa, I'm on my way to Alex's," I said, walking into the den.

"Here, Lewis, take my keys," my pa muttered, throwing his car keys to me without looking away from the television set.

"Are you sure, Pa?" I asked.

"Son, I trust you. Now go, make good decisions, be smart, and treat that girl with respect."

"You know I will, Pa."

"Goodnight, Lewis."

"Goodnight, Pa," I said, walking outside. I climbed into the driver's seat and drove to Alex's house.

She lived in an old shotgun house on a few acres of land just outside of town. Her father was a farmer who supplied produce directly to the Magnolia Market, the town's only department store, with clothing, groceries, hardware, furniture, appliances, and a laundromat. Her mother worked at the Magnolia Market in the clothing section.

I parked on the side of the street, and walked up to the front door.

"Hello?" a man asked, opening the door. It was Alex's father.

"Good evening, Mr. Keats, I'm here for Alex."

"Lewis! How wonderful to see you! She'll be ready in a minute. Come on in!" Mr. Keats said, pulling me inside.

"Good to see you, Lewis! How's your mother?" Mrs. Keats asked.

"Ma's been good. She just got a short-term job sewing the costumes for the community play. I'm gonna play piano in it."

"That's wonderful. We'll be sure to get front row seats."

"Hey, Lewis," Alex said, walking into the front room. She was wearing a dark blue dress and her hair was up.

"Hi, Alex, you ready to go?" I asked.

"Yes, let's go. Goodbye mother and father, don't worry, I'll make good decisions and be smart, and I'll be home at nine."

"Have fun Alex!" Mrs. Keats hollered as we walked out of her house. I opened the passenger door for Alex and walked to the driver's side. We drove back into town and I parked in front of the malt shop.

"Really Lewis? This is the best you can do?" she asked, incredulous.

"This is the first place we talked outside of school! Considering I can't break us into Magnolia High School, this is just the first of many places. Come on, I snagged us a booth in the corner," I said, dragging her out of the car. We ran inside and sat down in an empty corner of the shop.

A waitress came up with a full tray. She unloaded two chocolate milkshakes, two burgers, and two sides of fries. We ate our food and then she returned with a small white piece of paper.

"What is this?" Alex asked, picking it up.

"It's a clue. Andy wrote them while I planned the rest of the night. We're gonna have ourselves a little scavenger hunt."

"Sounds fun enough, what's our first clue?"

"*Right now you're at old Mickey's, but that's not the right place. Take a left at old Nicky Bellisario's house and stop where we hid in that summer rainstorm.*"

"I know where we have to go. Come on, Andy wants us to go to that old willow tree at the base of the park."

"Oh yeah! I remember that place!" I said, grabbing the car keys. I set a 20 down on the table and ran outside. We drove to the tree as it began to drizzle. Hidden in a knot on the tree was the next clue.

"*This is your second and final clue. I am now thinking of a place above you. I should know this to be true, you watched the fireworks with me amongst the dew,*" Alex read.

"The park!" I cried.

"Come on, let's go," she said, walking towards the car.

"Leave the car, come on, let's walk. It's a very beautiful night after all."

"Lewis! It's a downpour!"

"Exactly, it's a very beautiful night," I sighed, moseying up the hill. Alex chased after me and we walked up the hill hand in hand, getting more and more soaked.

At the top of the hill was a network of lights that had managed not to burn out. They led to an opening in the trees that overlooked Magnolia. Suddenly, music began to play. It was "Stand By Me" by Ben E. King, the song that Alex and I sang together three years ago. I smiled at her as we both began singing along.

The spell was broken when Alex said my name. "Lewis,"

"What is it?"

"We should get going. It's getting late."

"Oh yeah, I have to get you home by nine. Come on, I'll drive you home," I said, running her down the hill. We jumped in the car and I sped off to the Keats farm. When I pulled up, I saw Mr. Keats standing on the porch. We climbed out of the car and walked up to the house.

"Good evening, Mr. Keats."

"Why are you two soaked?"

"We were in the rain," Alex said. I nodded in agreement.

"Well, I should get going."

"Thanks for tonight, Lewis. See you Sunday?"

"Of course. Goodnight Alex, Mr. Keats, I said, walking through the soaked grass. The door closed.

"Lewis! Wait! I forgot something!" Alex cried, running out of the house. She ran into my arms and kissed me. "See you at church."

"Yeah, bye, see you at church," I mumbled, smiling sheepishly. Alex closed the door to her house.

"Yes!" I cheered, running to the car.

Chapter 7

New Orleans

Alex and I became a couple, and we stayed that way for a year.

She died two months ago in a car crash. It devastated the entire community. I wanted to marry her, and now that's never gonna happen.

We're graduating from Magnolia High School today, and I'm the Valedictorian. I don't want to stand up in front of the entire town. It's gonna be too hard.

I'm running away to New Orleans.

"Lewis! It's time to go!" my mother screeched from the kitchen. I tied my tie and put on my cap and gown. I grabbed my money off my dresser and the suitcase that was sitting by my door. I climbed into the car and we drove off to the high school. Andy and I raced off to our seats and sat down right as the ceremony began.

"Good morning everybody. I'm Mr. Greene, the English teacher, and I'm here to introduce a truly amazing individual. For the four years I have known this young man, I have known him to be incredibly strong. For two years, he and his family were prejudiced because of the color of their skin, and they were turned away at many places in town. This young man has overcome adversity and flourished, and he's always had music. When one of his good friends passed away this year, the first thing he did was play her favorite song on the piano and tried to remember her listening to it. Citizens of Magnolia, this young man is Lewis Ebbs, your Valedictorian. Lewis, come on up," Mr. Greene said, standing at the podium. I took a deep breath and walked to the stage. It's my duty to give a speech to send my friends off, and I might as well fulfill that job.

"Good morning, everyone, as you know, I'm Lewis Ebbs. I haven't prepared a speech for today because I didn't want to seem rehearsed," I started, leaning on the podium. "Ever since I was about three years old, music has been the most important thing in my life. It stayed that way for eleven years, until I met the girl who changed my life. Alexandra Keats was a wonderful person. She was kind, intuitive, and she wanted to change the world. I'm sorry she didn't get to make that happen. It's true that I played her favorite song on the piano when I heard she died. Alex was so similar to me that we had the same favorite song, 'Stand By Me' by Ben E. King.

"I understand today is about moving on, but I don't think I can do that until I find some answers in my life. Which is why this is goodbye. I hope you all have great lives, and if I see any of you again, I hope we still get along. Goodbye, and make sure to follow your dreams and all that jazz. Have good lives!" I finished, throwing my cap into the air. I tore off my gown, revealing an old suit, and I ran through the gym. Andy handed me my suitcase and I ran outside and down to the bus station. I hopped on a bus to New Orleans, and the first thing I did was get a job at a jazz club.

"What's your name, boy?" a tall black man asked as I walked in.

"I'm Lewis. I was wondering if you needed a pianist."

"Well that depends on what you can do. What can you play, boy?"

"Almost anything. Hit me with your hardest piece," I said.

"Anything? Play some Rachmaninoff."

"Is there a specific piece you want me to play?" I asked.

"Play 'Piano Concerto Number Three,'" he said.

"Okay, I can do that."

"You're not at all concerned?"

"No, my grandpa taught me Rachmaninoff when I was 14."

"Okay then, play the song."

I played the song with ease, and I absolutely blew that man away. He hired me and gave me a small bedroom above the club.

One year later, I was still playing piano at that club. Two years after that, I was still there. Nothing had happened. I wasn't getting picked up by any agents. So, on a rainy Monday morning, I bought bus tickets and returned to Magnolia.

Chapter 8

Take Me Back to the Good Old Days

I hopped onto the porch of my house and knocked on the door. My ma answered it. She was crying.

"Lewis? What are you doing back? I thought you were staying in New Orleans." she sniffed.

"Ma, what's going on? Is everyone okay?" I asked.

"G-grandpa just p-passed a-away," she muttered. I pulled her into a hug.

"What happened?"

"He had a heart attack, honey. He's gone! Oh God, he's gone!" she cried.

"Come on, let's go inside," I whispered, leading her in. Everyone was sitting at the dining room table. It was the most quiet my house had ever been. The only noise were the tears.

"Lewis? What are you doing here?" Andy asked, standing up.

"I gave up on New Orleans. I'm back for good," I said, giving him a hug. Andy was like another son in our family, so it made sense that he was here. We spent the entire night talking about Grandpa.

"Lewis, can you please play something? He loved your playing so much."

"Of course," I mumbled, walking over to our old piano. It was Grandpa's.

I stretched my fingers over the keys and began to play Bill Withers' "Lean on Me." When I got to the line, "You can call me brother," Andy stood up and joined in. As the song came to an end, I broke down in tears.

"Come on, you can stay at my place," Andy whispered, helping me stand. We walked across town to an old apartment building.

The funeral was two weeks later in the old funeral home. We just sang, like he would've wanted. That night, I moved into the apartment across the hall from Andy, and that summer, something strange happened.

Chapter 9

White Light

It was a balmy March day in 1975, and I was cooped in my apartment, attempting to compose the next great piano symphony, when I heard someone singing.

"Who's that singing?" I asked, looking warily down the corridor. Andy was standing in the hallway, listening.

"I don't know. I'm going to investigate," he said, walking down the hallway. I waited until he was down the last flight of stairs and proceeded down.

That day, I met a woman by the name of Lorraine Sky. She and Andy eventually fell in love and got married and had a little boy, and they were happy until they decided to get a divorce. Their son went missing, and that brought them back together. I remember Joey. He's a great kid. I remember what I said when I first taught him to play the piano.

"Now, son, I don't expect you to be able to play this at first, but with my help, you'll be the best piano player in Magnolia. This is my favorite song because it reminds me of your dad, my Grandpa, and the girl I loved in high school. I don't want you to ever forget this song. Let it stay with you until you see that white light. Joe, this what the best music is."

I said that right before I played "Lean On Me," by Bill Withers for him. That was before his sister was born. That was after I got married. That was before I died. Death is sort of interesting in a way. You never really think it's gonna happen to you until it does.

I died on a humid summer day during a rainstorm. I usually enjoy summer rain, but something seemed off about that day. I was heading back to my house after practice with the band which my father convinced me to join, when I heard a scream erupt from my small two-bedroom bungalow with a fiery red front door.

"Sandra!" I cried, running inside. The door had been flung open. My wife wasn't alone in there.

She was in our living room, standing behind the couch. Standing mere feet away from her was tall man so pale he didn't even look human. His arms were outstretched and his hands were holding a pistol.

"You son of a-"

"Shut up or I kill you both!" he shouted, trembling. He looked back to Sandra.

"Please, don't hurt me!" she begged, her fingers clasped together.

"It's too late. Your time has come," he said, beginning to pull the trigger. I pushed Sandra to the floor as a bullet erupted from the gun. I fell backwards, paralyzed.

I clutched my heart as my breaths grew to be few and far between. I saw a white light out of the corner of my eye. It seemed to be calling to me.

"Lewis, come, join us," someone whispered.

Alex, is that you?

"It's us, Lewis. You need to come with us," another voice chimed. It was my grandpa.

Don't worry, I'm coming.

The light grew larger and I saw them, standing in a

doorway, waving me over. I ran towards them. Sirens sounded in the distance.

"What's happening?" I asked.

"Lewis, you're dead. That man shot you," Alex cooed. She seemed oddly calm about this fact.

"What about Sandra? Is my wife okay?"

"We don't know what happened to your wife. The man took her. They've escaped the scene of the crime," my grandfather said.

"Come on, there's not much time. We have to deliver you to the Starkeeper."

We jumped through the doorway and into a world about as white as Magnolia when I first moved there. In the center of the landscape was a large throne, where a man was sitting. He walked towards us when he noticed me.

"Is this the man who was shot?" he asked in a calming voice.

"Yes, sir. This is Lewis Ebbs."

"Lewis. It is an honor to meet you. I have heard your music and it is by far my favorite. I am the Starkeeper. I keep the peace between mortals who have come to the afterlife. I am also a keeper of the stars."

"It is an honor to meet you, sir. But how did you know that I am a musician?"

"Lewis, I am Music. I am its essence, I am the one you first embraced when you were born. I am Music, and I am the most powerful entity ever created. Welcome to the afterlife, Lewis. We hope you enjoy our song."

I closed my eyes, and for just a moment, I felt myself slipping away into an old reggae song I tried out in New Orleans. I heard voices, but I couldn't understand what they were saying.

"The victim is a 35-year-old male, about six-foot-three. His full name is Lewis William Ebbs. He's married, but it's unclear where his spouse is."

I opened my eyes to see Music standing in front of me in a dark room.

"Good job. You have reached the first stage. Your heart and brain have shut down, along with some other organs, but you can still hear; although you cannot register in your mind what is being said. In about 30 minutes, you will not be able to hear, see, think, or move. You will be utterly defenseless, and at that time your soul will leave your body and you will become a ghost. Lewis, did you have any unfinished business back on Earth?"

"Yes, I lost my wife to that man who shot me."

"Lewis, I am afraid you will not be able to find your wife until someone living does. Because you don't know where she is, you will not be able to search for her. Do you have any other unfinished business left on Earth?"

"I never said goodbye to my friends and family. And I know my best friend will be dead-set on finding that man."

"Well, I can help you say goodbye, but I can't help you help your friend find who killed you. Follow me, we have to travel to the SRR."

"What's the SRR?"

"The Soul Retrieval Room. Yours should be coming through shortly," he said.

"Sir? Do have any name other than Music or Starkeeper?"

"Lewis, feel free to call me either of those names, or by Clef. Now, when your soul arrives, I want you to step on that platform and raise your arms upwards as if you are a bird about to take flight. Go on, stand on the platform," he said, pushing me towards a glass platform. I stood in the center as a small violet ball or light floated towards me. It shattered into a million tiny pieces when it hit my body.

I was back in Magnolia, standing in the funeral home.

"Lewis, you are now a ghost. Do whatever you must to give your loved ones closure, no matter how long it takes."

No matter how long it takes.

How long was this going to take? How long until I could rest in peace? The chapel doors opened and four men carried in a wooden coffin with another man carrying a box behind them. The men set the coffin down on a table in the front of the chapel and they set out a series of pictures and flowers. When they left, I walked up to the table.

It was my coffin. Those were my pictures, surrounded by an innumerable amount of flowers in vases. Sitting on a small raised table behind the coffin was a picture of me sitting at the piano next to a vase filled with white roses. The doors opened again and a slow procession of townspeople trickled inside the tiny chapel. These people were all here for the funeral. These people were all here for my funeral.

My breathing shuddered to a stop when I saw Andy, Lorraine, Joey, and Alex come inside behind my family. The crowd parted to let the smaller procession through. Andy looked worse than I'd ever seen him.

He was wearing a wrinkled suit and scuffed dress shoes. His usually clean-cut face had given way for a full beard and his eyes were bloodshot. They sat down in the front row and the priest stood in the front of the chapel.

"Citizens of Magnolia, we are here to celebrate the life of Lewis William Ebbs, a good friend to our town. I would like to welcome Andrew Grayson, his best friend to the podium to speak."

Andy took a deep breath. As he stood at the podium, I stood behind him.

"I met Lewis w-when w-we were e-eight-years-old. M-my p-parents always told me to b-be c-cordial to a-anyone, n-no matter what they looked like. Lewis and I became best friends within just minutes of knowing each other, a-and h-he was the greatest man I ever met, and that includes my f-father. You know what, I can't do this. I'm not gonna stand up here and tell you all my sob story about Lewis because he would've hated me for it. Lewis was shot in cold blood by a horrible person, and I'm never gonna give up searching for that person. I'm gonna avenge his death! I'm gonna get his wife back! This isn't over. It's not gonna be over until I say it's over!" he cried as Lorraine tried to pull him away from the podium.

Chapter 10

New Girl In Town

The year is 1979, and I'm 25 years old. Lorraine and Andy are married, and they have a son named Joey. They live in a small house across town.

That leaves me all alone. Except for one thing.

There's a new girl who moved into Andy's apartment. Her name is Sandra, and she's the newest Kindergarten teacher at Magnolia Elementary. I really like her.

"Come on in!" I shouted after someone knocked on the door. Sandra walked in, closing the door behind her.

"Hey, Lewis. Can I ask you something?"

"Wait just a second. I just learned a new song. You wanna hear it?" I asked.

"Sure, but can I ask you this question first?"

"Okay, ask away," I shrugged.

"Do you maybe want to go out tomorrow night? You know, on a date?" she asked.

"I'd love that! Yeah, it sounds great! I'll pick you up at seven?"

"Sure. What song have you learned now?"

"It's 'Joy To the World' by Three Dog Night. You heard it before?"

"Yes I have, Lewis. What's so special about it?"

"I made an acoustic piano version. It's really great."

"Well don't just stand there, play it!" she shouted. I sat down at my piano and began to play. When I finished she said, "That was amazing! Okay, I should go get my lesson plan for tomorrow."

"Goodbye, Sandra."

"Bye, Lewis!"

Sandra and I went on our date, and it paid off. We dated for four years, and in the winter of 1982, we got married at the church. We were only married for three years, and we weren't blessed with any children. I was killed before we could have kids.

Chapter 11

The Room

Suddenly, I was pulled away from the scene at the chapel and placed into a dark room with only the light of a desk lamp in the center of the room.

The door was forced open by a tall figure. He looked out from the doorway and gently closed the door and walked towards the light.

It was Andy. He looked like crap.

He looked worse than at my funeral, he looked worse than after Lorraine filed for divorce.

I shook my head and saw him pull photos out of a file folder and take a red ball of string from the desk. He walked over the wall and began pinning the photos to it.

"Oh my God…" I whispered, looking at the wall. It was almost filled with pictures and string and locations and maps. It looked like every detective movie I'd ever seen.

At the center of the crazy network was one picture torn in half. It was a picture from my wedding. Sandra was on the left, and I was on the right, with a red X over my face. I don't know what it means, but it can't be good.

"Okay, Lewis, let's start work for today," Andy said, connecting the new string with other lines of string.

"Andy… what happened to you?" I asked.

"Who is that?"

Andy could hear me. My best friend could hear me. This wasn't over, not yet. I could tell him that I was with him, and then I could help him track down the killer.

"That doesn't matter at the present moment. I need you to tell me something. How long have you been working on this?"

"For seven years. Who are you?"

Before I could answer, I was brought back to the afterlife. Clef was standing in front of me.

"Tell me, Lewis, why did you try to talk to your best friend? Do you want him to go insane?" he asked, his head in his hands.

"I wanted to help-"

"Lewis! You can't help! Andy needs to solve this case on his own. You can't help him at all."

"Why can't I help him? He needs my help!"

"Why can't you help him? I can think of about a million reasons as to why you can't help him, but reason number one is that he will be sent to a loony bin if you get in his way! Lorraine is already concerned about his physical health, but if she sees his mental health is out of whack, you're screwed!"

"Well, what do you expect me to do? Just be quiet and sit in the corner and watch him pin random pictures of me to a wall?"

"I think I have an idea of somewhere else you can go. You remember that young boy who you taught to play piano?"

"Joey! Yes, I remember Joey! How's he doing?"

"He's in Magnolia High School at the moment. He's in love with a dying girl, Lewis."

Chapter 12

The Innocent Girl

My face went blank.

"What do you mean he's in love with a dying girl? How do you know?" I asked, staring at Clef.

"I see everything, Lewis. I also know everything. Joey loves that girl, and it only took him five minutes of knowing her to fall in love. Come on, I'll take you there," Clef said, leading me towards a bamboo door. He opened it and I stepped into the auditorium in Magnolia High School. There was a red-haired girl singing on the stage, flanked by a string quartet.

"Good job, guys! Let's try 'Yesterday' from the top!" she hollered, her voice gravitating throughout the theater. I stepped to the side as the door opened and someone snuck in, eventually hiding in the corner.

It was Joey. He'd grown up so much.

As the song ended, he stood up and walked down the aisle, confident and the slightest bit cocky, just like Andy.

"Hey, you! Get out of here!" a blond-haired boy barked.

"Stand down, I come in peace," he said, putting his hands up. "I heard you in the hallway and I wanted to see the faces."

"What's your name?" the girl in the center asked.

"I'm Joe, short for Joseph. And you are?"

"None of your business. Can't you see we're in the middle of rehearsal?"

"Oh, don't worry. I'm a fellow musician."

"Really? Why don't you show us what you got?" a raven-haired girl asked.

"Sure, you got a piano or guitar anywhere?"

"Dude, the piano's right over there," a brown-haired girl said, pointing behind the group. He jumped onto the stage and sat down at the piano.

"You need sheet music?"

"Nope," he said.

He began to play the melody at the beginning of "The Stranger" by Billy Joel. He played and sang the entire song without making a single mistake. I should know. I taught him that song.

"What even was that?" the raven-haired girl asked.

"That would be a photographic memory at work," he said, tapping the side of his head. "And by the way, *The Stranger* is a better Billy Joel album than *An Innocent Man*."

He walked out of the auditorium, and I followed him, staying off to the side.

"You know, it wasn't nice to walk out like that."

It was the singing girl. She was standing in the center of the hallway with her arms crossed.

"Excuse me? I'm pretty sure your boyfriend wanted me out, so I left after I proved my musician status. It wasn't rude at all."

"Caleb's not my boyfriend. He just likes to think he is."

"Guess what? I don't really care," he said, walking down the hallway. He looked around and went into the music room.

He took out an electric guitar and plugged it into the amp. He began to play "While My Guitar Gently Weeps" by George Harrison, Joey's favorite Beatle. After he had finished the song he walked off to class.

"I've seen you before, Joe," someone said.

"Oh, you have?" he asked sarcastically.

"Yeah. you're always studying sheet music, but this morning was the first time I'd seen you play anything."

"What? It's out of the ordinary for a musician to study sheet music?" he asked, turning to see the girl walking up to him.

"I don't appreciate sarcasm."

"Too bad, I'm a very sarcastic person," he said, walking off.

I followed Joey home and I saw Lorraine pulling into the driveway of their house in her old blue Volkswagen Bug. She loved that thing. Joey talked to her for a short time and then walked up the stairs and into his bedroom. Suddenly, a small girl came bursting in. It was Alex. She definitely had Lorraine's looks. They talked for a few minutes about school and tests, and then they sang "Blackbird" by The Beatles. After Alex left, Joey sat back on his bed and quietly strummed some chords on an acoustic guitar. He was playing John Lennon's "Imagine."

I went through a couple weeks, just following Joey around, until one day, when I was brought back to the door with the White Light.

"Clef, what's going on?" I asked as he leaned out from the doorway.

"Estella should be coming through shortly. I want you to greet her."

"You mean-"

"Heart attack. She died almost instantly. Here she comes," he said, closing the doors. I saw her walking towards me, her red hair cascading over her shoulders.

"Who are you? Where am I? What happened?" she asked.

"Estella, I understand you were very close with my best friend's son."

"Are you Lewis?"

"Yes, I'm Lewis. Welcome to the afterlife, Estella. You died from a heart attack. Come, there is someone I'd like you to meet," I said, opening the door. I led her to Clef's throne.

"You must be Miss Estella James. I am the Starkeeper, and Music, among other things."

"It is nice to meet you, sir. Is there any way I can see Joe?" she asked.

"Yes, follow me. And Lewis, you come too," Clef nodded, walking through another unfamiliar doorway. "Estella, this is the Viewing Room. In this room, you can view anyone from Earth. All you have to do is say their name. I'll leave you to it," Clef said, leaving us in the room.

"Show me Joseph Grayson!" she shouted. The wall lit up, revealing Joey, collapsed against a doorway as rain pounded on the windows. It jumped forward to reveal him sitting on his bed, reading a letter.

The screen jumped forward again to reveal Joey packing a suitcase and grabbing a wad of money from a hidden compartment in his dresser. He hopped on a bus and rode to New York.

"He's doing almost exactly what I did in high school," I whispered, astonished.

"What did you do?"

"I ran out of my graduation ceremony after I delivered my valedictorian speech and hopped on a bus to New Orleans. I wanted to be the next great jazz musician, but I gave up after three years and went back to Magnolia."

A montage of events plagued the screen. He auditioned for a job in a club, he met a girl and they fell in love, he became famous, and he had a son named after me. His wife left him for her own career, and he was left alone with his little boy.

"He made it big," I whispered.

"I always knew he would. That boy had talent," Estella said.

"Show me Andrew Grayson!" I shouted. I saw the room again, and he was smiling, looking at a large picture of a man on a different wall with a red circle drawn around his face. It was the man who killed me.

Chapter 13

The Man Who Solved It All

"Lewis? Who was that man?" Estella asked as we ran towards Clef's throne.

"That was the man who killed me. Andy finally found him."

"Why is that so important?"

"That means my wife might still be alive! Clef! Andy solved the murder!" I cheered, turning to face him.

"So what you're telling me is that after 20 years he finally solved it?" Clef asked.

"It's been 20 years? How is that possible? I've only been here a few days!"

"Lewis, days melt into weeks, which melt into months, which melt into years, until you're left with a gooey mess that makes it unclear how long it's been."

"Well, can I see him? Can I see if my wife is safe?"

"Yes, you can go see Andy. But no talking to him this time. Good luck, Lewis, and be back as soon as you find that man. Someone very important will be arriving at that time."

"I'll be back as soon as possible, Clef!" I shouted, running towards the door to Earth.

I landed in the grass next to a very large house that had been abandoned years ago. It could've been a castle. I ran up to the house and saw a group of first responders carrying a body bag out of the house. They threw it into the ambulance.

Seconds later, Andy came out with a man in handcuffs. He threw the man into a maximum-security van, which would most likely take him to a maximum-security prison. My murder was finally solved. I noticed the window was open, so I put a piece of paper on the driver's seat.

I walked through the grass and got to the doors again. I waited there for the person who was supposed to be arriving. That was when I saw Sandra. She ran into my arms.

"Sandra… what are you doing here?" I asked, setting her on the ground.

"Well, I put up with that scumbag for years, because I hoped there would be a light at the end of the tunnel. There was no light, so, this morning, I climbed to the top of this insanely tall staircase that led nowhere in that horrible house, and I just- I just jumped," she muttered. "I missed you so much, Lewis."

"Come on, there are some people I'd like for you to meet," I said, leading her through the doors. I introduced her to Clef and Estella, and we all sat down together.

"So, how did you two meet?" Estella asked.

"Well, I had just gotten back from New Orleans, and it was after my grandpa's funeral and after Lorraine and Andy became a couple, that I met the newest teacher at the new Magnolia Junior High. We dated for a *long* time, and in the winter of 1982, we got married."

"It really is that simple." Sandra sighed.

We spent the rest of the day watching over Andy and Lorraine, making sure they were okay. We were doing just fine, watching and everything, when the screen switched over to show Joey, standing at the top of a building, poised to jump. Clef came into the Viewing Room.

"Lewis, I need you to go back."

Chapter 14

One Day to Save A Life

"What do you mean I have to go back? I thought that wasn't possible," I said dumbfounded.

"You have one day to save Joey's life and bring him back to Magnolia. Do you think you can do that?"

"I don't know, Clef. That sounds like a high demand," I sighed.

"You'll be alive temporarily. He'll be able to see you. Please, save this man. It's not his time yet."

"Okay, I'll go back."

"Good. Now, close your eyes, and imagine the very first piano lesson you gave that boy."

I closed my eyes. Suddenly, I felt the wind on my face and I heard car horns honking. I opened my eyes to see Joey walking up to the edge of the building.

"Now, son, I don't expect you to be able to play this at first, but with my help, you'll be the best piano player in Magnolia. This is my favorite song because it reminds me of your dad and the girl I loved in high school. I don't want you to ever forget this song. Let it stay with you until you see that white light. Joe, this what the best music is," I said, trying to project over the loud noise.

"Who's saying that?" he asked, turning around.

"It's me, Joey. It's your uncle Lewis."

"It can't be! You died!"

"Yeah, and I was killed by the man who kidnapped you! Joseph Lloyd Grayson, listen to me right here, right now. Do not, under any circumstances, take your own life. You have a son, for God's sake! Don't leave him alone! Have you even spoken to your family since you left?"

"No. I haven't had time. What are you doing here?"

"I was given the chance to come back for one day. I was given that chance because you were about to jump off a building! You need to come to Magnolia with me!" I cried, walking towards him.

"Why should I? You could be a figment of my imagination for all I care!"

"I'm real, Joey, but only for one day! You need to come with me!"

"What if you're lying?"

"I met Estella! She loved you, Joey! She still does!"

"Estella's dead! Where would you have met her?"

"In the afterlife! We're good friends!"

"I doubt that. Now, if you'll excuse me, I have something to take care of," he sighed, walking back to the edge of the roof.

In an effort to get his attention, I started singing Billy Withers' "Lean on Me" as I walked towards Joey. He stepped off the roof and gave me a hug.

"It is you! What are you doing here?"

"Like I already said, I was sent here for one day so I could save your life and bring you back to your family. Now, go get your son. We have to get you two back to Magnolia."

"I'll be right back," he said, running down the stairs. After a few minutes, he came back with a young boy.

"Lewis, this is the man who inspired your name," he said, kneeling down next to his son.

"It's nice to meet you, sir," he chirped, shaking my hand.

"So, how are we gonna go about this?"

"We're gonna teleport, of course. Clef, take us to Magnolia!" I shouted. We vanished from the rooftop and reappeared in front of Andy and Lorraine's house. I ran up to the front door and knocked. Andy opened it.

"Who are you? Lewis?" Andy asked. His eyes grew red until he was crying.

"I'm back, Andy, but only for one day. I'm with two very special people, too," I said, stepping aside to reveal Joey and little Lewis.

"Hey, Dad. I'm back for good this time."

"Joey!" he cried, running towards him. "Lorraine! You have to see who's here! Come on in!"

"Andy, what's going on?" she asked, walking into the living room. "Joey. And is that?"

"It's Lewis. He was brought back for just one day. And, this is our grandson."

"Andy, are you serious right now? You mean to tell me that our best friend, who has been dead for twenty years, is standing in front of us right now, and he's *human*?"

"Yes, that is exactly what I'm saying," he nodded.

"I don't believe it."

"Mom, it's all true. Everything Dad said, it's all true. I was about to kill myself by jumping of the ledge of a skyscraper, but Lewis showed up, and he saved my life. He came back to save my life."

"So it *is* true! Well, come on, Lewis! I bet it's been a *long* time since you've had a nice home-cooked meal. Alex! Guess who's here!"

"What is it, Mom?" she asked, coming down the stairs. If my math is correct, she should be about 22 right now.

"Hey, little sis. Meet your nephew," Joey said, lifting Lewis into his arms.

"Joey!" she cried, running towards him.

"And Alex, this is Lewis. He's your Dad's best friend."

"It's nice to meet you, Lewis. I've heard a lot about you," she said, shaking my hand. She looked even more like Lorraine now than she did when she was little.

"Come on, it's time for dinner," Lorraine sighed, sitting down at the table.

We ate a delicious dinner that Lorraine had made from scratch, and we caught up with each other, as if we were good friends who hadn't seen each other in a while. That really is what it was though. After everyone was finished, Joey and I sat down on the back porch to talk.

"Why did you try to jump, Joey?" I asked.

"Because I was done with everything. It's hard being famous. Everyone twists your words around, and you're either loved or hated. There's never any in-between. I just got fed up," he shrugged.

"Joey, that's not a good reason to attempt to take your own life. There's never a good reason!"

"Well, I'm sorry I'm not some hero like you were."

"Me? Joey, I wasn't a hero. I was never a hero no matter what I did. I couldn't save my grandpa, or Alex, the woman your sister was named after, or Sandra. I couldn't save any of those people. I was never a hero, Joey."

"You may not have been a hero in your life, but you were after your death. I can't possibly begin to tell you how many news articles I saw that were titled 'Local Man Dies To Save His Wife's Life.' You were the greatest hero in this town for so many years."

"I'm no hero now, am I? I'm just a dead man sent back to Earth for one day."

"You saved me. You saved someone's life, Lewis."

"Joe, your Mom wants you," Andy said, opening the door. Joey went inside and Andy sat down next to me, a beer bottle in his hand.

"What's it like, Lewis?"

"What do mean? What is it like being dead?"

"Yeah. What's it like?"

"It's like taking a break from everyone and everything until someone decides it's your time to live again."

"Is it - nice there?"

"It's the cleanest place I've ever seen. And don't worry, you can watch over everyone any time you want."

"I guess you're gonna have to get going here pretty soon, eh?"

"Yeah, I guess I have to."

"Come on, everyone's gonna want to say goodbye," he said, leading me inside. I said my goodbyes, and Andy followed me out into the front yard.

"I got your note, by the way."

"What note? I don't remember a note."

"Really? You didn't put a note in my windshield saying, and I quote, *'Please get better, I can't stand to see my best friend like this, sincerely, Lewis William Ebbs?'*"

"Okay, maybe I did."

"Of course you did! You signed your name, and your full name at that!"

"Bye, Andy."

"It's goodbye for *now*! I'll be with you before you know it!" he shouted.

As I walked down the street, I slowly began to disappear until I was back in the Afterlife.

Andy was right. Ten years after I went back, he died from lung cancer and joined me. I still remember exactly what happened.

"I told you it was just goodbye for now," he had said.

"It's great to see you, bud. You need to come meet Music. He's pretty awesome," I had responded.

When Lorraine died three years later, Andy greeted her the way I greeted him. When Joey died 50 years after that, we were all there to welcome him and introduce him to Clef. Once Joey joined us, we were put in charge of the Board of Music, which meant we were the first ones to find out if a newborn would become a musician or not.

Over a century after my death, I was brought back. I was reborn. Except I didn't exactly enjoy that family nearly as much as I enjoyed the life I left too early.

I tend to think of life as something that shouldn't go to waste. It should be an honor just to live for one day. I should know, that's what happened to me.

My name is Lewis William Ebbs, and that was my story.

Author's Note

    I always think of life as a song of sorts. It has its ups and downs, but it almost always strikes some chord in you that helps you feel better when you're sad, or gets your point across when you're trying to tell someone something.

    The reason I made these fictional lives revolve around music is because I do believe that it's the most powerful thing ever created. From Lorraine having a beautiful singing voice and Andy being skilled at guitar to Joey teaching himself on the piano when no one else could, and Estella, playing multiple instruments to take her mind off her health problems. My favorite main character in the book by far was Lewis. I loved writing his story because I could really insert my appreciation for music into his life.

    I wrote this book not only to show how we can affect others through our actions (for example Andy becoming sort of broken after Lewis dies), but to represent my love and appreciation for old music.

    Before we part ways, I want you to do just one thing for me. I want you to listen to "Lean On Me" by Bill Withers, and think of an important person in your life. Then, I want you to have a conversation with that person, whether it be face-to-face or over the phone. I want you to ask that person how their life has been going and what song they would use to explain their relationship with you.

I chose West Virginia for a setting because that's where Bill Withers grew up, and after hearing "Lean On Me," I knew it would fit perfectly with the storyline I was trying to develop. From there, I thought of a name for the small town, and I probably went through about 20 different names, trying to decide on the best one. I finally came up with Magnolia. It just fit.

Music strikes a chord in everybody, no matter what the song is about. Music is built off of emotion. After all, who would write a song if they didn't want to get a point across? For example, I'm a huge fan of Billy Joel's music. Whenever I listen to his song "It's Still Rock and Roll To Me," I think of how I get judged for my taste in music. Everyone either says "Oh, that stuff's boring," or "That artist/band sucks." But whenever I listen to that song, I understand that it doesn't matter what other people think about my taste in music. What matters is that I think.

You might be thinking right now, "Where is this going?" Well, I'm about to tell you why you should care about the music I like. The most prominent reason out there is that the music I enjoy inspired the music of today. Whenever you have a chance, I want you to look up artists who were inspired by The Beatles. I guarantee there will be at least 50 names on that list. I mean, why listen to new music when you can listen to what inspired that music.

Thank you for reading my book. I hope you enjoyed it.

SIGMA'S
BOOKSHELF

Sigma's Bookshelf (www.SigmasBookshelf.com) is an independent book publishing company that exclusively publishes the work of teenage authors, who are between the ages of 12 - 19. The company was founded in 2016 by Minnesota teenager Justin M. Anderson, whose first book, *Saving Stripes: A Kitty's Story*, was published when he was 14, and has since sold hundreds of copies.

"I know there are a lot of other teenagers out there who are good writers and deserve to have their work published, but don't have access to the kinds of resources I do. I wanted to help them," he said.

Sigma's Bookshelf is a sponsored project of Springboard for the Arts, a nonprofit arts service organization. Contributions on behalf of Sigma's Bookshelf may be made payable to Springboard for the Arts and are tax deductible to the extent permitted by law. Donations can be made online at www.SigmasBookshelf.com/donate.

www.ingramcontent.com/pod-product-compliance
Lightning Source LLC
Chambersburg PA
CBHW021023120726
47905CB00009B/3155